Other books by Sherrie DeMorrow:

Knight and Daye
Cloud of Dreams
The Elder Rose

THE ELDER ROSE

BY

SHERRIE DEMORROW

Published 2017 by

Lightning Source (UK) Ltd
Chapter House,
Pitfield,
Kiln Farm,
Milton Keynes
MK11 3LW,
UK

Cover Art Design by Sam Wall

samwall.com

To LL for help and support

To the memories of the various historical figures featured in this story

and in loving memory of AC, who continues to inspire my work

PREFACE

Please note **this is a book of fiction** and **NOT** meant as an accurate representation of historical events. The reader must suspend all preconceptions of belief in past history. There may be some reality in detail to it, but most of the scenarios are FAKE.

The historical personages of note (who were alive during the period written herein) were given some changes to their lives, but their memories have been respected. *No historical figure was harmed during the writing of this work.*

The historical attitudes towards sensitive issues, and people's prejudices of the time, had to remain intact to provide a sense of realism in the story.

Some place names given are **NOT** real, unless otherwise stated or recognised as real. Other characters (for the most part) are fictional and loosely based on people known of by the author.

Part I

William Alexander ('Willec') Woodes-Hastings

Chapter I

Totteringstate Hall loomed over the county of Woolanshire. Tall and imposing, it had been renovated in the late 1600s by my forebear, Charles Woodes-Hastings (the very same my father was named after). It still looked symmetrically squared with many windows and decorative bits and pieces, now featuring the latest classical style. There were hundreds of acres around us, with the local village a few miles past. The village, also called Totteringstate, housed our workers who made the estate profitable in the pig farming trade. The pigs and the farms remained in the county of Dumfushire.

We were not unlike many aristocrats who made a name for themselves just by trade, but also by name. The recent progenitor of our pig farming heritage, Roger Alexander, descended from the de Hastings line, which originated from Sur-Le-Merde, France. The 'de' bit was dropped sometime after the Norman Conquest to make it more Anglicised. The family itself had noble beginnings, lording over Sur-Le-Merde's pig farming community for a few generations. Our restless ancestor, William Phillip, landed in England with the rest of the Norman fleet and continued his position lording over his pig farm, which was revitalised in Dumfushire after the Conquest.

A few generations later, Roger's father, Roger William, fell into disarray. The family disowned him and then he had to conform to a peasant existence, having been knocked back down the social scale. He took up pig farming (*surprise, surprise!*) in the county of Dumfushire and started his way back from the bottom. As a fallen aristocrat, he had been able to marry whomever he wished for and did. He, at least, was allowed to keep the Hastings name, but without the privilege. Later on, his son, the aforementioned Roger, too, had the right to choose whomever he wanted to marry.

He married a lovely peasant girl, one Elizabethia Mary Woodes, and he thought it would be a good idea to double barrel the names. However, as he was the son of the fallen, the maid he married had taken some precedence over Roger.

Hence, the name became Woodes-Hastings. Roger continued the pig farming trade as a proper living and got himself in a right state in the mud. Yet it did pay off, because through it, he turned around his fortune. Even though he was a fallen branch of the Hastings tree, he planted his own roots and created the little 'dynasty' of Woodes-Hastings.

Although we were pig farmers ourselves, the business has grown considerably since my medieval forebear started it up back in the day. We now lorded over the farmers themselves (*coming full circle*, I might add), who toiled with the animals, making them fit for food and profit... and they were happy doing so.

He built and lived in Totteringstate Hall in the county of Woolanshire, to keep separate his private interests from the business. It was so named Totteringstate because the motto for de Hastings was 'Tout L'Estate' (from the French, meaning 'all the land or estate'). The estate was not as grand by today's standards, yet at the time, it kept a medieval charm about it through the next few centuries until Charles began implementing the classical touches upon it.

Overall, my immediate family were a friendly lot and could not be snobbish. There were little bits of rebelliousness in our blood, but it never took over our lives. Our very origins had gone against precedence, so that norm became our norm. We were a close knit bunch, consisting of my father Charles, my mother Hermanda, a twin brother Lancelot John and a sister Emmadayle, who lives with her husband, one Captain Greyrivers, in Sydmouth Harbour where his ship, the HMS Dockmore resides. In addition, the Captain had a brother in the Army.

The air was good out this way, with a taste of saltiness coming from the nearby coast. It reminded me that Sydmouth itself (never mind the harbour) was not far from here; a town built up along the river Syd.

There was a slight mist, too, as I perused the estate with total fondness and glee. It seemed a dreamy landscape, worthy of a Gainsborough. It was ideal, compared to the soldier's life I led for many years...

I was a veteran of North American colonial conflict, the late Seven Years War, which I was glad to be rid of. It was bloody, confusing, conflicting and an overall horror. I honestly detested the colonies whose inhabitants thought they knew better than the rest of us. They knew they were British, (either by blood or just by living in our colonies), and subject to our culture, our language, our laws, and our religion (but there were choices regarding the latter). Ironically, most of them came from the peasant classes of Europe and even Britain. Only a few (*and I do mean a few!*) came from our circles. They all had a mind and will of their own. Yea, they claim it was sound... *more like the sound of a trump from an elephant calling for its food and/or mate*, I thought in my silly manner.

As I stood upon the grass, I watched a bird fly to a nearby manor house in the distance. The house straddled our border, but we allowed the family to buy that part of our land for their estate. It was not sprawling like ours, but it was surely not pale in comparison.

Greystone Estate housed the family Asboathe, whose daughter, Daffnette, was promised in marriage to me when she came of age. I sighed when thinking about her because, due to my military career, it would be difficult to keep such a promise to one so young and wishful. When I returned home from the late colonial War, I was expected to do my duty and marry Daffnette. However, I asked to put it off indefinitely, as I was called away on other military assignments in the meantime.

I was also aware of trouble brewing again in the colonial realm.

It had been nearly fifteen years... Since we had won various, formerly French controlled territories in Canada and North America, we expected the colonists to be thankful.

To our surprise, they were not. They argued and argued about taxation, went about protesting and causing difficulty for our officials in charge. I found it intolerable that the colonists, whilst proud to live under our banner, refused to pay a small amount toward the cost of the previous conflict. *Wars do not pay for themselves, you know*, and, as we did them a service, they returned the favour with ingratitude. I figured I would get a call-up to serve in that hemisphere, *again*!

So, no Daffnette for now, I feared. There was no room for romance during a bitter conflict, even if it involved *other* people. I bided my time and prayed, yet knowing the inevitable.

* * * * * *

As I sat in my study, smoking my pipe, a bell went off. Probably a lazy relative needing to unbuckle a shoe and is too fat to do it himself, I sniggered. Then, a chime dinged the coming of the hour. *So many minutes past the hour...* I sighed and carried on reading.

A voice from behind the door called. 'Willec?'

'Yes, what is it?' I gave no notice and continued my worldly perusal.

'A letter for you, sir.'

'Put it in the folio, that's a good girl,' I replied. It was Fantasie, a slave who my brother- in-law salvaged from a group destined for the Caribbean.

She came into the room in a respectful manner, put the letter where requested and left the room.

I sighed again and grumbled to myself, *Who is it now? Another appointment*, I reckoned. *Maybe it was from...*

I took the letter from the folio and broke the seal formerly burned upon it. The seal wasn't much; it was just a good way to show who the sender was and to keep messages private.

Dear Willec,
Shall we to dinner? I want to be in your company again, before service claims you for another, and possibly the last, time. May we make it tomorrow for five in the evening? I love you very much and hope for the day we can finally be wed. Yours faithfully and Ever fondly, Daff xx

Daffnette... Daffnette. My mind swirled in a haze, thinking of that girl the next estate over who has her sights on me, and was willing to wait. Me. Why? The Asboathes ran the textile mills in Woolanshire and settled into the estate next door to ours. I found them to be social climbers of the middling sort... those who wanted to get ahead in life by marrying a local 'name', if one understands the idea. Our name goes back centuries. Her family was of the nouveau riche and now that they made their money, they buy up or build their own estate and marry into old blood, like ours.

Daffnette was a pretty sort, but unfortunately dull-in-mind. She would bore the prickles off a hedgehog. Her mindset was very worldly (*but not worldly-wise, I'm afraid*) and fashionable, yet she tried to compensate for it. When she did, however, it was all too catastrophic to bear.

I really wondered if I were to take such a lady for a wife. I personally did not like her, as I was a man-of-the-world and have been around the block a few times. I knew she loved me; she always stated so in her letters, including this most recent message. Yet, I cannot see myself reciprocating the favour. Love between families was negotiable; one married for convenience, i.e., money or alliance. In my experience, life was too short to muck about with worldly desires. *I wanted to believe in love*, and as much as I felt Daffnette would make a good bride for me, I personally had my doubts.

Another knock came at the door. *Was it Fantasie again?*

A blonde coloured head poked through the door. My twin brother Lancelot John made a kindly appearance.

'Willec,' he greeted.

We embraced as brothers do. Between us, I was the smart one, but a bit less spiritual than he. Lottie entered the cloth and managed the local parish church in Totteringstate village. He was slightly taller than me (but not by much), with a plain look which bespoke his profession. His eyes were an expressive dark blue and he never wore a wig as he felt it was difficult enough to tame his own shaggy mop.

'So did you get called up yet?' He anticipated my recall as much as I did. However, I had other plans.

'Yes. Yes, I did,' I stated teasingly and deadpan, 'I am wanted by appointment.' *I surely wanted to wind Lottie up.*

'When will you leave us?'

'Well, the letter here tells me about five in the evening.' *I enjoyed this.*

Lottie could not take it any longer. It looked as if he was bursting at the seams.

'Tell me where. I can go with you to see you off. Is your uniform ready? Will it still fit you? It had been some time, you know.'

I smiled a cruel smile at him. 'No, it does not fit. It is a different War this time, isn't it?'

Lottie pouted, 'I did not know Totteringstate Regiment changed its uniform.'

I felt I had to put the poor man out of his misery. 'Well, if you must know, I will be going to a dinner tomorrow evening at Greystone Estate.'

It dawned on Lottie who it was. 'You're seeing Daffy,' he cried in realisation. 'How could you... to lead me on like that!'

'"Tis what brothers do... especially twins.'

'Will you still wear your uniform?'

'Certainly not. I will impress her with *silk o'shears*... I shall be on the cutting edge for her. Let us see if she can keep up.'

'Ah, but a girl just loves a uniform,' Lottie argued.

'This one does not. The moment Daff sees me in such garb, despite its said good looks, I fear it might upset her. She is as anxious for my eventual call-up as you and I. As of yet, my papers had not arrived!'

'She is hung upon you, no?'

'Like an ancestor's portrait upon these walls, Lottie. Heavens, we were promised to one another at one point, but I confess I really do not think I can love her. She is worldly, as am I, but in a different and (to me) disagreeable way. My military career has taken precedence over the relationship and I firmly believe it would not be fair upon the lady to wait for my return... IF I return.'

Eagerness betrayed my twin. 'If Heaven wills your removal, Willec, can I have her?'

Oh, Lottie, you cheeky bastard!

'I do not believe she is the religious type,' I said.

'No. I suppose not.'

We paused and left it there. It was not worth her coming betwixt us... especially since she *was* promised to me.

Tonight's dinner bell sounded and we left the room together to gather for our evening meal. It will be another twenty-four hours before the real gong hits.

Chapter II

The next day, I awoke to chirping birds and low baying livestock from a neighbouring farm a fair distance away. A few minutes past, there was a knock at the door. I stirred further.

Fantasie came in. 'Your father wants a word with you. Please come down for breakfast.'

'Yes, yes,' I spoke impatiently, 'Tell him I will be there as soon as possible.'

Damn, what did Father want?

I hastily put on a pair of breeches which hung from the back of my desk chair and added the other bits of apparel before heading out toward the dining room for a morning meal I may well wish to forget.

The walk down the corridor from my suite was pleasant enough. The walls were covered with ancestral hangings upon gold leaf wallpaper. There were floral vases and other chintzy finery originating from the East, mail ordered by brother-in-law Greyrivers. I descended the winding staircase, lined with a solid oak rail as I made my way to join the rest of the Woodes-Hastings clan who resided within these walls of Totteringstate Hall.

'Willec, you're here, at last,' Father exclaimed.

'I could not arrive unsheathed, could I?' My retort was playful, with no disrespect intended.

We sat down, began with a quick prayer supplied by Lottie and commenced eating. A while later, once all the edibles were consumed, and we were having our tea, Father engaged me.

'So, I hear you have an appointment at Greystone Estate later this evening.'

'Yes, Father,' I affirmed sheepishly.

'You better make a good impression on Daffnette. We wished you together for many years. She is of marriageable age now and I firmly believe it would be better for you to tie the knot.'

I felt saddened Father was still pursuing this line of thought when I told him otherwise. *My military career came first. I expected to be recalled into service.*

'Charles, please don't goad the boy on,' Mother piped up in my defence.

'Hermanda, the boy is nearly forty years of age,' Father argued, turning to me, 'Aren't you?'

I sat silent, hating the juvenile treatment I was getting from him. *Me... the war hero, back in one piece, fighting for King and Country.* I firmly believed Father needed to get his priorities straight. After all, there is Lottie to consider, just as marriageable and possibly more agreeable to the same.

Father continued, now acknowledging my chosen profession, 'Well, my boy, you've been a soldier and served your country well, but damn you, William Alexander, it is time to settle down. Look at you, you are so past it, my boy, past it!'

Mother put her hand on me. 'Ignore him son. Do what you feel is best for yourself.'

I knew what was best, I reckoned, and that was not to break a promise. Especially so because someone's heart was involved.

Daffnette was much younger than me by about fifteen years or so, and a nice girl, but I did not want to commit. I could not commit. *Not now, anyway.*

I outwardly sighed, drank my tea and excused myself. Lottie sat at the table silent and Mother and Father carried on with their business. I was not trying to run away but I needed to preen my emotions before they got unruffled again, *possibly later on...*

Evening came. I made my way, in my flashy suit and britches, toward the carriage. *I will keep the appointment, but I would not make more promises.* I felt I was in a quagmire and I did not wish further entrenchment within. However, it was I who was invited to supper with the great Daffnette and I could not let her down.

Greystone Estate was slightly larger compared to good old Totteringstate. We had beautiful gardens, carefully manicured and lovingly managed. There was much space for a good runabout and a folly to rest against when one had run the course planned. The Asboathes decorated their gardens with water features, greenhouses (*to grow one's own*, as they say), flowers blooming everywhere and the manor house itself was just as grand.

Yea, Greystone Estate was for the up-and-coming and it showed. We at Totteringstate did not have to produce anything for show. *Our history told all...*

I left my carriage and walked toward the entrance. A few children were playing nearby, past the stone urn that decorated the front portico. I wondered from afar if they were family members or visiting friends. I figured they could not be Daff's because she was still a maid, yet.

One of the girls looked up. I peered ever so closer to her and realised it was Daff's cousin, Brette.

'Willec's here, Willec's here,' she shouted like musket-fire. *It was a strain on the ears,* I could tell you. *So much for a quiet beginning.*

Daffnette came out in all her finery... a silken blue dress, patterned with a floral design (akin to those vases I saw back home) with silver buckled shoes... and her hair, piled high.

'Willec,' she greeted and gave me a kiss on the cheek. 'It is so good of you to come to us, at last. Thank you for accepting the invite.'

'You're welcome,' I said as she beckoned me inside.

I was led into a smaller room, which looked very snug. I guess it was where all Daffnette's friends would settle before the evening meal, or otherwise (*the latter, I had to reflect upon*).

We sat down on one of the exquisitely decorated sofas, a Chippendale, I believed, when she asked, 'So, how's your family?'

'Doing well, thank you,' I droned. My mind laid elsewhere but I needed to concentrate on the matter at hand. I had to tell her my real feelings toward her and the likely possibility of the call-up. I feared it would break her heart and she'd fling me aside like a torn dishcloth a servant would use. *Would I truly care? Maybe she will find someone else more suitable?*

'Daffnette, I have something...,' I was rudely cut off.

'Oh, have you seen my new dress? Mother bought several reams of fabric in London on a recent trip and made this dress for me. I went with her and do you know, the shoppes are filled with so much stock from abroad. Gosh, it was so stylish, she just had to buy some of it. Isn't it just fab?'

'Scrummy, ma'am,' I jested. I stared at her. She was beautiful. The dress she wore was well suited to her majestic figure. *However, my immediate future may lead me to...*

'Willec, would you like a drink?'

'Thank you.'

'Anything in particular?

'Whatever you are having, my dear.'

'Good, I will see to it.' She left the room and left me to my thoughts, as tempestuous as they were. Her fashionable concerns and enthusiasm had come at a bad time. *I had to tell her.*

Daff returned with a couple of glasses of wine and gave me one. I sipped some, watching her sit down as she guzzled hers.

She remarked afterward, 'Wow, that was a buzz, wasn't it?'

'I would not know. I take in my drinks very slowly.'

'So what was it you wanted to tell me?' *Ah, you remembered, Daff, after the rude interruption.*

I cleared my throat and put the glass down, *dishcloth at the ready...*

'Daffnette, you know I may be recalled soon.'

'I know. That is why I had invited you over, so we can see each other before you leave us.'

'You do realise I am not going abroad on holiday or for training exercises. There is a very real possibility I may be killed. I honestly do not want to make a promise to you and leave you, unfulfilled.'

I sucked in my breath and continued, 'It would not be fair to you and not right, in my eyes, to see you fix your star onto mine. You should allow yourself to choose whomever you wish and not wait up for me, for I might not return.'

There, I laid it onto her. Let's see her drink herself out of it!

'So, you would not consider me to be your wife?' Her eyes began to walk the path of sorrow.

'As I said, it would not be fair, would it? Now, if I do return, and we are both free to one another, there may be a consideration due. On another note, I can imagine yourself being attached to another whilst I am gone and my heart would be broken upon my return. Would you entertain that?'

She paused and agreed with my logic, 'It would be pretty rotten, I suppose, but you will not be let off that easy!'

'Well,' I smiled and put my arm around her, 'We will see about that. There is my brother, you know. He is unwed and runs the local parish.'

'Yes, I know,' she recalled, 'Yet, he is a man of the cloth and a clever one indeed. I am no match for him!'

'And you think yourself a match for a soldier? A match that may never be? At least no one would be firing rounds at Lottie.'

'True. He may live longer, but I love *you*, Willec.' She gave me a pouted look.

'Yes, I know of your love for me. That is why I cannot let this continue. I do care about you very much and do not wish to see you hurt.'

'I appreciate your sentiment towards me, but I prefer yourself to your brother.'

'He is the safer bet, my dear. Look, I did not come over to exchange cruel words with you. If this be our last meeting, let it be of fondness. I wanted you to know how I felt, despite everything and it would be a most painful loss, if...,' I trailed on a bit, as I gathered the good Daffnette in my arms to hold her. She continued to pout at me.

The dinner bell rang. I looked up at the clock. *'Twas the hour of six, and this was going to be a long eventide...*

We said our goodbyes a few hours later and a horse was provided for me to ride back to Totteringstate Hall. As I galloped into the late evening's dying sun, I reflected on the time with Daffnette and I was plenty certain I was correct in my thought. Summertime has its pleasantries, but here, there was none that inspired.

I made my way to our grand Hall when I saw brother Lottie sitting on a bench outside (*it was a salvaged pew, actually*), reading his prayer book. He sat still, closed-eyed in prayer, focused on his God. Then, in returning to his book, his eye caught a glimpse of my horse's bridle.

'Willec,' he stood up excitedly, putting down his book with respect, 'How did your evening go? I was waiting for you and praying with bated breath.'

'Lottie,' I stated, dismounting, 'You may exhale now. The time there was well spent, albeit sadly spent.'

'Oh?'

'I had to let her down a bit. Told her what likely may happen.'

'Still unwilling to commit? Father will be none-too-pleased.'

'Well, Father has his own life, and I have mine. Daff is a wonderful girl, but she seems an unlikely match for a soldier like me. I suggested to her you may fit her bill.'

'Wait a minute, Willec...'

'You confessed an interest earlier on!'

'Well, I did not wish to seem wanting.'

'Look, we're both gentlemen and know what we want out of life, for now. Things may change, yes, and that is why I feel so strongly about you having her. You would be the safer one compared to me.'

'Just cos I am not getting shot at all the time!'

'That is exactly my point.'

'So you think she would be good vicar's wife material?'

'I believe she is cut from the very cloth!'

I smiled cruelly at Lottie, but I felt my idea was for the best.

'She is a bit dull, don't you think, sir, and very worldly.'

'All women are like that,' I dismissed.

The sun cast its final rays upon our day. The opportunity was there for Daffnette to consider. She said she loved me, though, so it will be interesting to see how the barge floats. I sighed and asked a grounds man to deal with the horse. Lottie and I went inside for a good sleep.

Chapter III

Upon my paper's arrival in the past month, I received a visitor at Totteringstate Hall. It so happened to be Major General Wolfe-Harris, officer of the 12th Regiment, Totteringstate. He had just been to the colonies awhile ago and returned with salacious news regarding the same.

When the Major General arrived, I had on my uniform from the previous conflict. I hoped it would show my continued interest in my career and make a good impression on him. This was not Daffnette, but someone of far greater significance.

Fantasie answered the door as Wolfe-Harris stepped in, wiping his boots upon the mat used for said purpose. He was tall, dark hair yielding to grey, and an overall comely appearance but for brown eyes showing bags of character the size of Daff's last shopping spree.

He entered the parlour where I was waiting for him. I stood up and greeted him, 'Major General, sir, it is good to see you again, for it had been far too long. How have you been all the while?'

'Fine, but most unsettled,' the officer began, 'The colonists are starting to revolt in the most violent manner possible and I heard there had been a struggle recently in the outskirts of the colony of Massachusetts. I returned as soon as I could because we will need reinforcements and fast.'

I reflected upon this. A few years back, it started with protestation of a leftover tea tax (*we were hoping to get away with that*). The tea that we shipped there was subject to a major atrocity which involved it being cast into the surrounding harbour. The intentional destruction of King's property made my blood boil. *It really did hurt.* The action showed such lack of respect for our law and way of life that it seemed they wanted nothing short of independence.

Independence. Blah, what a word! God forbid. Such arseholes, I tell you.

'Good gosh,' I exclaimed, 'So we are to be called up to snuff out the rebellion and reinforce our rights over theirs.'

'Indeed so, and consider yourself called up. I am sorry it came suddenly, but it could not be avoided.'

'Actually, I expected this. I am not offended.'

'Well, good. We have been ordered to New York.'

New York...Oh God, why???

I groaned and my heart was heavy. We passed through there on the way back to England (well, it was a port city after all!). *Jesus, what a nightmare.* There was a multitude of many nations which emigrated there (which made it too crowded for my taste!), the streets were reasonably clean but narrow, and to confuse the matter further, various houses of worship reflected the Protestant German, French, and Dutch settlements there. There was a synagogue amongst them, too. However, the city was also known for being anti-British... I've heard the Sons of Liberty had a branch office there, so-to-speak and their actions were screaming to be quashed. *My God, my God, have you forsaken your dearest servant? I know I am a servant of the Crown, fighting (and gloriously, I might add) for King and County, but....ugh....*

I further groaned. 'New York, eh?'

'New York, Colonel,' Wolfe-Harris confirmed.

I sighed.

The Major General took notice, 'Is that a sign of trepidation?'

I squirmed in my seat, crossing my legs and eventually exhaling, 'Yes. I was lucky in the last War. Now, I fear my time may be up. I had not prepared, really.'

'I understand.' Wolfe-Harris, mostly impatient to do his duty, had a sensitive side.

I went on, 'If I die in service, *over there*, would you see to it I get a burial in Totteringstate Parish? I so hate to be done over abroad.'

'Circumstances permitting, I will favour your request, Willec.' The Major General was good like that.

I sighed again, this time of relief. I did not care about Daff anymore. I just needed to concentrate on the upcoming task ahead. To go *there*, quell the rebellion (reinstating Royal authority), and return home.....and *maybe* marry Daff. *Yet, as I am a soldier, this may not be.*

A soft knock was heard at the door. My brother Lottie peered in with concern. *He so cared for me, bless him*, and asked, 'You alright?'

The Major General did not hesitate, 'He will be fine,' he then observed, 'You must be his brother.'

'Yes. Yes, I am. His twin, Lancelot John.'

'Your resemblance is striking. Just don't pull a fast one on us and put yourself in Willec's place.'

Lottie laughed, 'Sir, I would not dream of it. My inadequacies would shine brighter than the sun if I were to take my brother's place in your regiment. My business is with the Lord and only the Lord. I do not wish to fight in any war. And besides, his boots would be a size larger than mine. That would make a difference.'

'It would, indeed,' Wolfe-Harris laughed, 'Good to meet you, Vicar.'

'Likewise, and I wish you luck abroad.' They shook hands and Lottie departed the room.

'Nice twin you've got. You close?'

'Closer than you think,' I said.

'Umm...it would be a shame to be lost.'

'Yea, 'twould be amiss.'

'Now, about our mission,' Wolfe-Harris got to the bottom of his visit, 'As stated earlier, the bulk of our troops will land in New York. Some of us will travel slightly north of the City to Scatsville. There is a girl in the area who is loyal to us but her family, the Havènots, is associated with the rebels. In fact, the grandfather is part of the Sons of Liberty. He is also predominant in the Jewish community and is helping fund the rebellion. There is much stirring of the masses against us. I believe he has been chosen to be a delegate in their 'supposed' Congress or whatever the hell they call it.'

'A superstitious lot of backwater, backstabbing ingrates, more like. Jewish, you say?'

'Unfortunately. She hates it and it shows. The family adopted her after the mother died and had been bullying her over the years to conform to their ways; but they cannot admit to doing so, due to their prominence. There is a back story as well, but we will discuss that bit later. The real problem is the family itself.'

'Pardon for the interruption, Sir,' I interjected, 'but how old is the lass?'

'Got to be late teens, give or take. Looks younger than her years, but she can take care of herself. The grandmother, in particular, is very overprotective of her and is holding her back. She, with the rest of the family, are trying, forcibly, to convert Cynthia into the rebellion as well as reinforcing their religion upon her. Cynthia resists them as the colonies are resisting us, but she is not one of them. They are of a False Nation and are Purveyors of Vile Impotence. We need to get her out of there so we can deal with that seditious family before the Rebellion spreads toward the outer colonies. If that happens, we've a powder keg on our hands!'

Wow, this looks more compromising by the moment.

Wolfe-Harris continued, 'There is an Indian tribe who live nearby called the Catatoahs. Their Chief, called Crazypaws, is willing to help and side with us. He even proposed a raid on the community to help get the girl out. Their previous leader, Forepaws, had given in to the Jews' request for the land (to build their community) and accepted their offer. Crazypaws is livid about this and wants the land back for his own tribe. I will detach a small unit for you to command on this northern campaign.'

'Yes, sir,' I groaned a bit more. Now we are dealing with more than the rebels and matters that really do not concern us (*which will have an effect on our plans if left unchecked*).

I then asked, 'So when do we leave?'

'In a few months. Hopefully by year's end, though it will be a rough crossing. Depends. It may be as late as February or March. You will be notified accordingly. In the meantime, you are to attend training exercises to refresh your memory and to get refitted for uniform. Our colours are slightly outdated.'

Well, it had been nearly twenty years since the last time, duh!

'Sir, if I may, I certainly do not wish to be out of fashion.'

'Compelling, and witty,' Wolfe-Harris smiled, 'Hopefully, we will be successful. The King will do anything to end the conflict. This rebellion is doing His nut in.'

'And that of many politicians on both sides of the pond, I can assure you,' I soothed jokingly, but with intention.

'Your father's an MP for Totteringstate, isn't he?'

'I can confirm the same, but he does not discuss matters of state at home, as I do not discuss anything of the military nature.'

'A wise move. Alright, I must be going, now. You will be hearing from my subordinate, Greyrivers, who will instruct you accordingly.'

I stood up, and saluted my superior, 'Yes, sir. Thank you, sir.'

'Godspeed, Willec. You're a good soldier and may His Mercy shine on all of us in this crisis. Your brother can pray for our endeavour.'

'Sounds good, however, I had not reckoned you to be a religious man, sir.'

'I am not, but every little scrap of divine justice can assist in such matters, plus we could be fighting the Devil himself, it seems.'

'Fantasie will see you to the door. I trust we will not meet again until we leave.'

'Maybe sooner, one never knows. I always check up on the regimental exercises, remember? I might pop in one day.'

'Yes, I know you do so for security purposes.'

'Right. Fare thee well.'

'Goodbye, sir,' I said as I opened the door for Wolfe-Harris, and Fantasie led him to the front door.

I sat back in the parlour and pondered. New York? A young lady to rescue from a rebellious family? Heavens, could she be our ally? It was stated in our meeting she hated her family and proved herself loyal to the King. It was something worth considering. *If anything, I prayed she would not be as dull as Daff.*

Chapter IV

Weeks later, I found myself outside on the parade square of HQ in a nearby hamlet of Silarby. The sun was out and it was cool and crisp in the air. The smoke coming out of my mouth was far from its pipe back at Totteringstate. Many hours of training went into us soldiers and I met up with some I was familiar with during the previous colonial conflict. I sighed and carried on with the exercises. Buckingham was having a problem loading his musket. *Poor man, as if he had not remembered the last time.*

'Here,' I offered, as I showed him the loading procedure, again.

'Why thank you, Willec. I do not know what I would do without you. It is a wonder I am still alive, thanks to you.'

I blushed. I helped the dear boy from an enemy attack near a deer field in the wilds of, oh, what-its-name? I could not recall the place. Mostly Indian territory and many namesakes of the lands we fought upon are not easy upon the English tongue to pronounce. Anyhow, I honestly hate to bring forward such memory, but for the sake of my dear friend.

I finished the demo and watched Bucks have another go. He was aging, bless him, but we needed the men to fight on.

''Ow's that, Willec?' Buckingham believed he caught on.

'Good. Now, keep practicing, laddie,' I commanded, with affection.

Another hour passed. The exercise was at its end and Sergeant Clarence dismissed us, with emphasis on the drill to practise at home.

Nay-Smith, Cateliffe, Buckingham and myself packed up and went off to our local.

I asked Clarence, 'Willing to take horse with us, sir?'

'Splendid. I will see you shortly. You go on,' he replied.

'Right-o!' It was nice to be mates with those on the high-up.

I clicked my tongue to signal my horse, Leader, to ride out toward Totteringstate. The terrain was pleasant enough, mostly dirt roads, for anything harder may hurt the horse's feet. I continually prayed as I passed through the countryside, fearing these last moments may be my last view of such beautiful territory.

We later met up at the pub, *Under-the-Castle*, and had our drinks as usual.

* * * * * *

Our regiment boarded the ship, the HMS *Going Places* for the several week odd journey to New York. It was long, arduous and unfortunately my close mates and I did not have much to do, except heave, play cards, drink rum and do whatever was available on the ship. Some of us were so bored, we even helped the crew in their tasks!

Once we entered the realm of the New World, we disembarked the ship. It *was so long ago since I was last here*; upon my departure, I had forgotten its bustling environment. *I must have been in the foliage of Totteringstate far too long.* There were so many people in New York, and, as crazy as it was, it seemed like a nice place on the outside. Living there, however, proved otherwise....

As my fellow soldiers and I had marched through the manic atmosphere, my attention was pressed to find a group of people walking together... *looked like a family of some kind.*

There were, what I assumed, a matronly woman, several younger (but full-grown) adults sharing a similar generation and an 'odd-one-out', who was much, much younger... *I reckoned she could not be more than twenty years old.*

I found that young girl staring at us. I was nay offended, for I was used to being stared at. All soldiers are... especially with our uniforms. I stifled a giggle. *What female does not like a uniform... unless she stepped or slept on the wrong side of one.*

A loud, shrill voice (in the manner of a fishwife) had permeated my ears.

'Stop looking at the soldiers. How dare you lay eyes on such nonsense? They are gentile scum,' it stated with resolve.

This must have been the grandmother I had been warned about. Oh God, what a formidable woman... and what a shouty voice! Ugh! It was the Havènot clan, who were quite prominent in the political and religious scene in their respective community. Perhaps this was the lass referred to in conversation with Wolfe-Harris, earlier at Totteringstate. The Havènots had business to attend to here in New York; Scatsville was a long way away.

I tried not to stare too keenly as I continued on with my group on the path assigned, as we passed the family.

Another voice piped up, 'What are you looking at?' *God, another shouter.* It came from the eldest grown-up child. Some of our eyes did wander, I guess, but we did not expect to receive the brutal welcome.

One of the other members of the family took the wee young girl and huddled against her as to block her further view of us.

It was a shame because I liked the look of the girl, and needed to study her face to be able to retrieve her from that horrible bunch.

I chanced another view of her, which thankfully I'd gotten, and moved along with my group. We continued the march and were billeted in reasonable quarters in the surrounding outer district. One of our party met with a local contact from the Catatoahs, who were long-term allies of ours. I was particularly fond of Chief Crazypaws and looked forward to our meeting regarding our mission.

Upon arrival to our quarters (it took time to get there!) within this pernicious isle (yes, New York was an island, Manhattan Island, as it is otherwise known), we stuck it out for several days before our mission was to be fulfilled. The quarters were purpose built (used by the Dutch in an earlier day), and practical. It was definitely not as fancy as Totteringstate, but not as squalid as a slave's lodgings. Cateliffe, Nay-Smith and Buckingham were roommates with me and we passed the time together playing cards, smoking pipes (even sharing them when one of us ran out of tobacco!) and doing our drills to keep fit for the mission's run. As a personal aside, I took along a miniature sized Bible, which comforted me to no end.

Later on, once refreshed, ready and horses provided, we embarked on our mission to Scatsville. The Catatoah camp was a few miles out of the town limits, surrounding it like a hawk trying to retrieve its prey. Apparently it was like that because Scatsville used to be the Catatoah's home until... I tried to remember what the Major General told me about the history. *Sigh.* *It never seems to work out for anyone over here. Someone always gets shafted.* Crazypaws and his people did not deserve such treatment. They assisted us in the previous War and we became good friends ever since. So this needed resolving, and *it all amounted to that one wee girl I saw by the quay.*

The area we rode in was largely untamed, but for a few Indian villages, including the Catatoahs, peppering the landscape.

This was most familiar to me, as the foliage was as thick as in Totteringstate. Green, earthen, floral, natural smelling and wild animals were aspects that kept my mind in touch with home.

Soon after, we were greeted with the meowing of a little black and white cat, wearing a collar with three bells. It was as if he was expecting a batch of British soldiers come scampering through the land. The kindly animal led us toward a small camp a few feet away and I soon recalled the area from before.

A tall, tan skinned man, fully clothed in ceremonial garb, came out of his teepee. It was Chief Crazypaws and my gaze upon him was in awe.

'Willec,' the Chief greeted.

'Crazypaws, so good to see you again,' I shook his hand, 'I brought some fellow soldiers and friends of mine.' I introduced everybody to the good Chief and they all greeted him warmly.

'Would you like a meal, you look awfully tired.'

'It had been a journey, and a half,' Cateliffe whinged.

'Good, we will see to your needs and prepare for our raid.'

I felt it was best to inquire of the young girl we saw by the quayside.

'Yes, Willec, you had seen the girl in question,' Crazypaws confirmed, 'Did you hear other voices?'

'Yes, the grandmother and elder daughter, I believe,' I said.

'Those two are the worst. She was bullied again?'

'I do not know about that, all I heard them say is to stop looking at us.'

The Chief contemplated. 'There ways are not our ways, nor are they your ways. Theirs is a narrow path to walk on. It is not an easy path and much of it conflicts with outer society. My grandfather, Forepaws, saw them with a sympathetic view in his mind and allowed them to have our land. We live on the outskirts, surrounding the town... but we want that land returned to us. The community has become corrupted by their own traditions and they think like a wheel heavily ground in dirt. Heaven help one to go outside the wheel track.'

I thought about Crazypaw's view, which was sound to me. He was of a good mindset, educated by and in the wilderness, and gave out philosophic advice. *Just as a leader should.*

'I heard the grandfather is big in their camp,' I spoke in his terms.

'Ah yes, very big. He is away at the moment. In a congress. Out of state. Philadelphia, I think. That is where they meet now and again and I think this time, they're dreaming big. We must retrieve that girl. She might know or have heard more. At least their pestering of her will end.'

'No one can stop us. After all, it is our Empire we are defending.'

'Could be a lot more, too.'

I had to admire the Chief. We ate and talked more before settling in for the night. Further plans were made for the upcoming raid. I prayed hard it would work, for there was much at stake.

Chapter V

The next morning, all was not well in the Havènot household. Although Cynthia had been exposed to the outside world before, she was awestruck by the soldiery she saw recently. The grandmother was none too pleased and angry that Cynthia was starting to pull away from her family and their way of life. Now was a bad time and the grandfather, Mr Havènot, had been away on business and was not to return for a while. There were secret meetings he attended in Philadelphia which brooded complete discretion. Thus, he remained away.

Cynthia sat at the table eating whilst other members of the family were preparing for their Sabbath. They practiced the Jewish religion, but they were not Jewish by origin. About two generations ago, their forebears, (whose name remains unknown to history, as it had been changed without authority), had lived in a small village on the western side of Germany. The original respective families were Catholic, but also unknown. Their two teenage children fell in love, without their parent's consent (due to their age and class). One day, they hatched a plan to escape their families and run off together to get married. However, if caught, they would be sent home. So, they ran off from village to nearby village, eastward, to try to break the ties that bore them. They went as far as the Polish border, even crossing it and travelling crazy therein.

Parochial law at the time insisted a church marriage must be done for permanently settled residents of the town... not for people 'on the run', or newcomers, so to speak. There were no civil registry offices to speak of and everything (it seemed) revolved around religion. The runaway couple had money, using it for travel and food. They stumbled across a synagogue and thought maybe they could get married there... if they had the money for it. Based on the *assumption* the couple were Jewish (and they did not tell him otherwise), the rabbi there married them and the couple paid the fee. At last, they were legally untied from their old families and most eager to begin new lives with this... *religion*.

It is not known as to how they 'learned' about Judaism, but they went to various synagogues along the way of their travels. Eventually, they left Europe itself, wanting to be as far away from their old lives as possible. The ship first went to England before heading off to America. The young couple felt England was too close to home and notably too Christian which went against their new-found *religion*.

They landed in America and somehow ended up in New York. The couple began a family there and joined the local Jewish community. Some bright spark felt it necessary to live up North of the city, in a place more pure and isolated from gentile folk and other outside influences. They chose land belonging to an Indian tribe called the Catatoahs, whose leader at the time, Forepaws, had allowed the community to purchase the land from him. The community was then called Scatsville because they told the Catatoahs to 'scat' away, once the land was purchased. There was no love lost between the two parties and grudges began to form in the Indian's psyche.

Cynthia had finished her food in quick-time when someone took the plate away, quite hastily, and scolded, 'You should not eat so fast. Not good for you.'

'I can't help it,' she said, 'Snatching the plate from me doesn't help, you know.'

Well, that was that, Cynthia sighed. She got up when the grandmother called her over.

'What?' Cynthia wanted to return to her room, sulk and read.

'I did not like you looking at the soldiers yesterday. I told you, they are a menace to us. That is why we live up here, away from such gentile scum.'

That name-calling burned in Cynthia--she hated her family referring to everyone else as such. *Not them, oh, no, God forbid!*

'So what if I do look at a soldier. They have their orders. They are interested in following only them, not women.'

The grandmother continued the scolding and finger pointing, 'You are so naive. You do not think for once they would try to take advantage of a young girl? Huh??!!'

'And what of it? It is not like I am attractive enough to make them want me. You'd seen to that!'

'We were only trying to protect you from harm; they may get fresh with you.'

'Why? You think I am feeble or something?'

'There is something about you that is not right.'

'Yeah, I know. I am not fully Jewish. My father was Italian Catholic and YOU cast him out into the street, denying me a father and your daughter a good husband.'

'HE WAS NOT JEWISH!'

'I am entitled to my father's heritage. I do not see why I have to follow yours. You are not even real yourself!'

'I WAS RAISED AS JEW. MY MOTHER WAS A JEW, I AM ONE, MY DAUGHTER IS ONE AND NOW *YOU* ARE ONE!'

'By origin, you were not, and what is more, YOU SNUCK IN, assuming your *so-called Jewish identity*. You are a FAKE and living a lie.'

There was a pause when the grandmother got up and slapped Cynthia in the face.

'HOW DARE YOU CALL US FAKE! YOU ARE NOTHING BUT JEWISH. YOU ARE NOT PROTESTANT, YOU ARE NOT CATHOLIC, YOU ARE NOT ANGLO-SAXON. YOU ARE A JEW. ONCE A JEW, ALWAYS A JEW.'

This really hurt.

'One day, I will leave and do what I want in life.'

'You will not, you will remain with us until you get married. IF you get married. There is that lovely boy, Geoffrey Claude Jacobson. We arranged for him to visit in the coming week, so you better be on your best behaviour.'

'And what if I refuse.'

'YOU WILL NEVER REFUSE US. YOU WILL REMAIN WITH US ALL OF YOUR DAYS. YOU THINK YOU CAN BE INDEPENDENT, BUT YOU DO NOT KNOW HOW. I DARE YOU TO EVEN TRY IT. YOU'LL NEVER AMOUNT TO ANYTHING ANYWAY.'

The berating continued for some time. The arguing began with them since year dot. Cynthia had never, at any time, gotten along with her family. She was an odd piece of a weird puzzle and she knew it. She also wanted *out*. It got to the point where she began to cry and stormed out of the main room into her bedroom at the back.

The grandmother continued her rant, 'YOU UNGRATEFUL CHILD, AFTER ALL WE'VE DONE FOR YOU SINCE YOUR MOTHER DIED!'

Another female relative, the eldest daughter chimed in, 'You are a taker. We are a family of givers and you are a taker.'

Another daughter quipped, 'You are a selfish pig!'

Both daughters returned to their tasks.

Cynthia sobbed further. Her soul was tormented in the most cruel way and psychologically, there was no escape from it. This went on for years. Her mother died recently, unable to care for Cynthia due to epilepsy. There was a small relationship between them, in the meantime, but the grandmother supervised it, making it difficult for Cynthia to get to know her natural mother properly. She never even knew her father, all she knew was the surname Silardicus. A surname she was born with and entitled to, as a heritage, but even that was snatched away (like a dinner plate) when the grandparents took over Cynthia's life. They adopted her swiftly into the family, changing her name as such, in the hope of expunging any connexion to her non-Jewish heritage.

The day was long for Cynthia. She remained in the room and was badgered several times to help out with the Sabbath preparations. Of course, she refused, which angered the grandmother even more.

'YOU MAY STAY IN YOUR ROOM BUT TONIGHT, WE WILL BE GOING TO THE CENTRE FOR SERVICES AND YOU ARE COMING WITH US!'

The grandmother had odd ways of reference.

Cynthia begrudged, 'FINE, I'LL GO!'

There, just to shut that bitch up!

She wandered in her own mental garden when she decided to pray. This was an odd thing for Cynthia to do, but she secretly wanted Christianity as her religion. As her father was a Catholic, she felt entitled to the same. She hated being Jewish, and the abuse and boredom she received from its way of life, was unparalleled to reality. *She knew the grass was greener... elsewhere, and she wanted a piece of the action.* The torment in her soul festered like an old wound. There was an English text of the Old Testament she had, but it did not console her. *There was more to the story than this, and that bit I need to read about.*

She looked around and went on her knees next to her bed. Jews did not normally pray kneeling, but she wasn't having any of that!

'Lord,' she said, 'I hope you are listening to me at the moment, for I am in great need. I have put up with this hurt for many years now and I believe I can look after myself. I no longer wish to remain in this family nor wish to remain within the stifling confines of their *religion.* You can see they do not love me, unless I conform to 'THEIR' beliefs. *You and I know it is false and they are living a lie.* Please, God, help me learn the Christian way and comfort me in this distress. I enjoyed looking at the soldiers. I did not do it to defy anyone, but between you and me, I think they are a far better option, especially compared to that Jacobson character they want me to marry. *They* are real men. That Geoffrey is a fucking *drag.* I've met him and was not impressed. I do not want to be committed to someone I do not love. I know there is another person for me and if so, a good man and a Christian. Preferably a British man... one of those soldiers might do!? *I wish to live my own life* and not live through someone else's eyes and for other people, being told what to do. I was a child when things were made difficult for me, when that grandmother took over my life. She seeks control of me to ensure this evil lie continues and is passed on. We cannot let that happen.

'May the truth be known and may Your Will be done... and done to me, if You are kind enough to allow. Amen.'

Cynthia got up unto the bed and laid upon it, quietly daydreaming of potential love; with her bedroom door shut and none to disturb her...

...at least not until the evening.

Chapter VI

Our little group of myself, Cateliffe and Nay-Smith remained overnight with the Catatoahs and the rest of the regiment stayed in the barracks. We stayed in our own tee-pee, cleared for our visitation. It was a peaceful night, with further catch-up chat with the Chief and a nice game of cards, which he enjoyed with us very much. We were used to sleeping rough, and Crazypaws had a thought.

'Would you like one of our women for your company?'

I considered the idea, but my heart remained on the task of rescuing the Havènot girl... I could not get past it.

'It is most kind, but not for me, thanks. Perhaps one of my men would like to, erm...,' I answered, with a look at my fellows.

'Yes please,' Cateliffe showed no restraint... *Silly Cat!*

Nay-Smith was slightly abashed, but veered toward the trajectory. 'Yea, I'll have one too.'

'Right, that's settled. Willec, if you change your mind,' Crazypaws further offered.

'Thank you,' I was starting to regret my decision of refusal, but I found a way out, 'Maybe later.'

The Chief left us to fetch the ladies.

'You wally,' Cateliffe chided.

'Think you are so godly, eh? Just cos you're brother's a vicar!'

'Nay-Smith, get over it,' I shouted. *God, what a whinge.*

'We know you are horny,' Cateliffe teased cruelly.

He was right... I was, but I did not want to let my guard down with a lady... *not just yet.*

My men later received their respective women, even swapping among themselves. I scoffed and read my Bible. I do confess to earthly desires, but I felt bound to my duty to set an example, even if the others did not comply. As it was just the three of us, and, as I was their leader on this mission, I decided to do what was best for me.

I slept fitfully, as it had been some time I *roughed* it. Being a soldier was hard work and one does not expect to be in a fluffy accommodation all the time, even as an officer. Yet it was difficult to get used to sleeping on the ground, despite the comforts available to us by the Catatoahs. They were simply just... different. It was nothing more and there was nothing wrong with it.

The next morning found my colleagues most satisfied, snoring away like the drunken, horny elephants that they were. I did not find such luxury, so I sat outside on a small makeshift chair, awaiting for sunrise. It was a most beautiful sight, especially when one is outdoors. One could feel the cool of the air and the emerging light that brought hope to failing dreams.

I sighed again, missing my life in Totteringstate, my family, and possibly Daffnette (*though the latter took much deliberation*). I was intrigued by the Havènot girl. Gosh, I forgot to ask Crazypaws her name. *Shit, I must remember.* I spent some time studying her face, it would do me good to be able to address the same.

By mid-morning, the four of us had breakfast and spent the day at the Catatoah camp, planning for the raid, as well as indulging in some outdoor pursuits, like hunting.

It was afternoon. The day flew by quite pleasantly and I really enjoyed my time with the tribesmen. It was nice to take our coats (and wigs) off for a change and it seemed we may get to keep them off for this raid.

There was discussion about how to approach and Crazypaws had an idea.

'It is end of week, yeah? A Friday... the girl's family attends some kind of worship, with the rest of the community, in a building not far from here. We attack then.'

I suddenly remembered the all-important question, 'Chief, what is the girl's name?'

'Cynthia. Cynthia Havènot. That is all.'

'Much obliged to you,' I winked.

Cynthia... ah, nice... I was beginning to succumb into further desire.

The community apparently had a building, a temple or what-not, and every week, Friday and/or Saturday (I think), they go there for prayer. I could not imagine what it would be like, *but I bet it was borne with much endurance.* For one, I knew their service was not in English.

Crazypaws continued, 'The advantage to the attack tonight is the whole community attends this worship and we can distract those present to retrieve the Havènot girl. I will assign this to Willec. The rest of you shall enter the building from all sides to surround all there. You will need to blend in with us, so you must discard your British coats and dress like us, yeah?'

Ah, we disguise ourselves as fellow Indians. *Now, this will be interesting.*

'We go and change,' Crazypaws beckoned, 'My men will find suitable skins for you.'

'Thank you,' I replied, 'I guess I will need to attract the young Cynthia.'

'I have got just the kit to do it,' Crazypaws returned the wink, 'Come with me.'

We conversed further, and later, we dispersed to prepare for the raid. Cateliffe and Nay-Smith got into their respective gear and they looked the part. I, however, was treated otherwise for this special occasion. I had put on buckskin trousers and shoes they called moccasins, but was told to withhold the shirt. A tin of tan coloured paint was used upon my person in the most unceremonious way and brushed into every crevice of my pasty-coloured flesh until *I* looked the part. I also had to apply face paint, along with this tan foundation (to make it consistent). Once I was made over, I looked in a small looking-glass (reserved only for the Chief) and was aghast. *They made me over all right; I looked like a totally different person.* I so wished Daff were here to see this, so I could amuse myself watching her freak out over my personage.

I turned to Cateliffe, 'How do I look?'

'Splendid. You'll do. Maybe this Cynthia will find you attractive, once she finds you are not an Indian.'

'Yeah, right. Save my uniform for me,' I called out.

'It'll be here with the rest of ours. Let's go.'

We filed out of the camp to find that temple earlier discussed. As I was delegated to rescuing Cynthia from the misery we tasted recently, I needed to put my mind to it.

Crazypaws came up to me, 'You could be happily mistaken for one of us. You look quite keen and may make a decent catch.'

This was encouraging.

'Pray we do not go amiss,' I begged.

'I, too, keep in touch with the Great Spirit above,' he smiled.

Onward we went, walking quietly and calmly. I'd guessed it must have been a good half-hour's walk or so (I left my pocket watch behind, obviously) and I confessed fatigue. *Never mind,* I went on.

Eventually, we found the building where we heard a noisy din. Many voices were singing or chanting in unison (typical of any service, really). *Ah yes, I was correct in remembering their Sabbath services. Good time for a raid.*

Crazypaws gave the signal. 'Ready... GO!'

We all hastily ran into the building as the raid commenced. There was shock and awe in response to the chaos that usually accompanies a raid. The Indian kit we wore hid our British identities, as it was felt it would make more sense to be consistent when working with our allies.

My eyes carefully scanned the room. *God, too many backs of heads with coverings of some sort. That will not do.* I moved closer toward the front, deflecting those trying to prevent my purpose. The room lit up with fear as many of our party had commenced the violence we had planned.

I hoped I could find this girl soon so we can make our escape. I believed I spotted the family. *Umm...no grandfather there... ah, that's right, away on business.* He was important and I wanted this secrecy to be disclosed to me.

Very soon, I heard shouting similar to the style I heard by the New York quayside. The resonance was stifling and I had to concentrate harder to get past the harshness.

'Stay with us, Cynthia, do not look around,' the grandmother shouted over the chaos.

Cynthia looked around anyway, as her fascination got the better of her. She did remain with the family, appearing scared. I saw someone placing their hand on her shoulder. *They are certainly clamping down on her.*

At last, I was able to make my move. I asked Cateliffe, who was beside me, to distract the family, especially that grandmother. He agreed and went into action. The hand was released away from Cynthia, as Cateliffe took the person next to her, and slit her throat with a small knife (provided with the kit he wore). I then wrenched Cynthia away from the dying relative, and gave her over to Nay-Smith, who hustled her out the door. I took out a tomahawk (kindly provided for me too) and went for the grandmother. It was sad I had to bear witness and mete out the execution; yet, I believe this is what Cynthia needed to rest her soul. So, I snuck up from behind and grabbing the woman's (if one can call her one) hair in a bunch, I pulled it back and used the tomahawk to scalp the head. I took another weapon out of my other pocket, which was a blade of some kind, and I beheaded the Medusa that plagued Cynthia's life.

Cateliffe led the rest of the family into the centre of the room, who was screaming by this time, seeing their matriarch dead on the floor.

I took the head and put it in a bag I used for supplies. I wanted to prove the loss was complete.

I ran out, whooping like the rest, for the disguise's sake. *Truthfully, I sounded like a blithering idiot.*

I met up with the dear girl and Crazypaws outside. Nay-Smith and I had a hug together.

'Here's the girl,' he said.

I turned to the sweetness in front of me, 'Sorry I was delayed, but I do have happy news.'

Cynthia was astonished and looked squarely at me in a calm moment.

'You dress well, sir, for an Indian,' she mocked.

Did Cynthia find my disguise transparent?

I had to confess. 'Erm, no, I am not an Indian. I am English. My men and I had dressed especially for this occasion.'

'Great place to do it, I guess,' she replied, fingering the area around my navel and watching the paint reveal my true colour, 'So what is the news?'

I felt a whirlwind of affection, but not now. I had a duty to perform to her.

I took the deadhead out of the bag. 'Behold, your torment is at an end. You will not be needing this.' I dropped it on the floor.

Cynthia bent down to peruse the head. *Yep, it was her, all right.*

I saw the look of relief on her face and asked, 'May we dispose of it or would you like the honour?'

'Let us see what the Chief wants,' Cynthia replied.

I met up with Crazypaws, with Cynthia standing beside me.

'I got her,' I triumphantly announced.

'It looks to me she got you,' he replied, pointing at the finger marks which removed some of the paint off my tummy area, 'What have you there, Cynthia?'

'A prize, courtesy of this gentlemen here,' she pointed at me and showed Crazypaws the head.

'My condolences... and congratulations on your triumph.'

I blushed. I so wanted to kiss her and Cateliffe's previous comment at me could get stuffed in the wind. *If only he could see me now.*

The Havènots, by this time, were devoured by the crowd of Indians and worshippers and could not find Cynthia. They called and screamed her name, but to no avail. She was already outside by this point and in *our* care. My men and the other Indians of our party, who survived, had returned outside to us for further instructions.

'Get the shutters closed and doors locked. We will burn the place down,' the Chief ordered, 'Cynthia, give me the head', which she happily provided.

'That will teach them,' I quipped.

The Indians went about the final touches of the plan. My men and I began to light torches with Crazypaws.

Cynthia watched with no remorse to the fate we planned for the people inside, including her family. She hated them all with every fibre of her body. *After all these years, now, it is time.*

She asked, 'May I help light the torches?'

Crazypaws' eyes lit up, 'You do realise what you are about to do?'

'Yes, sir,' she stated with confidence, 'Please give me a torch. I will end this befouled existence once and for all. Are you with me?'

The Chief and I stared at one another. Her defiance toward her own was not what we expected. But hey-ho, it gave us an advantage and those people being 'her own' was obviously in question.

We were joined by the other Catatoahs, who ensured the place was secured inside and out. They began to make torches for themselves which blazed alight. I acquired a torch for myself and Cynthia.

'Here's to a new beginning for you, my dear,' I said.

'Here's to a better life, perhaps with you,' she replied.

Crazypaws gave the word, 'Let's get our lands back!'

We accompanied the others with torches. Crazypaws still had the dead grandmother's head in his possession.

He turned to Cynthia. 'Here, my girl, this is your fight. Begin the annihilation.'

'With pleasure,' she cooed, taking the head, ready to set it ablaze.

I gave my torch to Cateliffe as I grabbed a large rock, which could break windows. I realised the shutters were secured, but I asked Crazypaws get one of his men to reopen at least one of them so I could dispose of the trophy head for Cynthia. We will not be needing *that* anymore.

'Sure thing. You go?'

'Aye,' I admitted, 'I'll do this for Cynthia.'

'You must really like the girl,' the Chief noticed.

'I'm warming to her,' I smiled.

The shutter was opened and I threw the rock with all my strength. Geez, I never did this before, but it felt good to really let my raw emotions rip, even if it was for the benefit of someone else. The glass yielded to my rock, then I asked for the head.

'Sir, here it is,' Cynthia said, handing it to me.

She set it alight and again, my strength was put to the test as I threw the thing back where it belonged. My men and Crazypaws' had gone off to commence the building's destruction. Yes, it did matter there were people in there. Yes, they were not all responsible for the hurt inflicted upon the dear Cynthia. Yet, it was something that had to be done to set an example to others (*especially in respect to the sedition they emanated*), as well as to help my friend reacquire his old lands back for his people.

The building had taken to the fire, which carried on its natural course. It was easier that we got them all in one place and any lingering survivors can be dealt with by Crazypaws' tribesmen (once the land had been resettled).

Crazypaws saw the glee in Cynthia's face, but felt concerned for the girl. 'Where is your house, so you can retrieve what you need? You will not be returning here again.'

'I will show you,' she called out, 'It's not far from here.'

She went up to the Chief and personally thanked him for all his help. She gave him a hug which he returned to her.

'You go with God, my child... or at least these British officers. I think one of them has a shine for you.'

Now it was Cynthia's turn to blush.

'I believe so too. I do appreciate your time and assistance. It was such an unruly existence,' she sighed.

I asked, 'They were really not your people, were they?'

'No. They chased my natural father away and I heard he died not too long ago.'

'That is too bad, Cynthia,' I sympathised, 'But we can lament and brood later. There is work to do.'

'Right-o,' she said as she thrust herself onward, as we walked to her place.

Chapter VII

The house was located in a row next to the end one in the distance, which was getting nearer as we pursued the path trodden. It was detached and of a similar design to the others. To me, it was nothing special... I knew of these houses and this one was mediocre compared to ol' Totteringstate Hall. To Crazypaws, who spent all his life in tents and tee-pees, it looked substantial.

'Wow, that is some tee-pee!' Crazypaws was amazed at the sight in front of him.

'Yes,' I observed. *That grandfather was important and it showed.*

'I do not have much. I lived in the spare room and it should not take long to sort out,' Cynthia stated.

'You go in. We wait here,' Crazypaws answered.

'I would very much like you to accompany me, sir. Please?' She pointed at me and I agreed.

'We won't be long,' I uttered as I followed her inside.

It was a nice home, comfortable and not wanting in good taste, but for heretical religious emblems scattered about in decoration. She went toward the rear of the place.

'This is my room,' she invited me in.

'Nice. They treated you well, then,' I noted.

'Not really, sir. It is a long story and time is not on my side to tell it to you right now.'

'Accepted. Get your things. You are leaving.'

She took out a small suitcase and began to pack some essentials, which included some clothes, a book or two, and other sundries. It will be a long journey for her.

I felt embarrassed that she did not know my name, though I knew hers. We had been hastily introduced during the raid, and I felt, during this down-time, I would introduce myself to her.

'My name is Colonel William Alexander Woodes-Hastings. My friends, and all who know me, call me Willec.'

'Ah, good to meet you, at last, Willec,' she shook my hand and carried on packing, 'I like your pet name.'

'Yes,' I reflected, 'The others do too and it stuck on me over the years.'

'Where in England do you live?'

'I live in Totteringstate, Woolanshire. It is the seat of the Woodes-Hastings. We own the lands therein.'

'Wow, a real aristocrat!'

'Well, we have our history and go back centuries.'

Her packing was done but she paused to reflect.

'I guess the Indians can take over, I will not be returning nor needing this ever again,' she lamented.

'No, you will not, but you will enter a better life.'

'Oh?' She seemed keen.

'We will discuss it later. Crazypaws is waiting.'

We walked out the house; she, with suitcase in hand, had an idea.

'I was wondering, Willec, since no one will return this night, why not bed down here? I mean, why camp out in the dirt, when you've got, um...,' she gestured toward the house.

'Splendid idea,' Crazypaws agreed, 'Our people can stay in these houses for the night. You and Willec's men can stay at your place.'

'Great,' Cynthia was excited.

She was right. *No one would be returning to them.*

'We'd better get inside,' the Chief sensed,' It looks like rain.'

My men returned inside with Crazypaws, who arranged sleeping quarters for all of us amongst the housing on the block. Cynthia, myself, and the rest of my team remained at her place, whilst Crazypaws and some of his folk tried it out at one or three of the other houses. He never experienced civilised life before and wanted to have a go in a different sort of environment.

We said our goodnights and went into our respective places. Crazypaws sent one of his men, Runnamoke, to fetch our uniforms from his camp ground, and he dropped it off where we stayed.

'Ah, the uniforms. Thank you ever so much. It has been a good raid,' I said to Runnamoke, as I had him place the uniforms and accompanying gear on the large sofa in the lounge.

'No problem. Yeh, good raid. Make for fine evening. Good to sleep by. Until morning,' he said, shaking my hand and departing.

Cynthia's home was very adequate for Cateliffe, Nay-Smith and myself. We could each have private room for ourselves, but as we were close friends, and wanted to initiate Cynthia into our group, we picked the largest room. The master bedroom was extreme, to say the least. There were relics from the past, but nothing worth our reckoning. Cynthia had her gear and maybe tomorrow will find more to bring with her from her room that she did not pack previously.

We settled in for the night on the nice super bed that lay before us.

'I do not think it would be right if we all share this bed. Nay-Smith and I will go into one of the other rooms. I have a feeling you both are going to wish for solitude,' Cateliffe suggested.

'I thank you for your kind consideration, Cat, and I believe, too, it would be for the best,' I looked at Cynthia, who wholeheartedly agreed.

'Well, as you wish. I take my leave and pray you sleep well tonight.' Cateliffe went to join Nay-Smith toward the pick of another of the rooms.

'Now, then,' I cooed, 'We are alone. You scared?'

'No,' Cynthia said, and she lunged at me with an emotional kiss, which I gathered was a thank you to me for all we accomplished today.

'I do not mean to intrude, my dear, and if you do not want to tell me, you needn't, but, do you pray at night?'

Cynthia pondered... 'Not as often as I would like. As I do not follow the religion that family coerced me into, I want to learn the Christian way. Unfortunately, I am ignorant of such things.'

'In that case, we will leave that for now, and I will pray for you. It is not difficult, and it will not take a moment.'

I closed my eyes and knelt beside the bed. I kept silence as the thoughts of the day flowed out of my soul and (hopefully) unto Heaven's lap. I begged forgiveness for those I had killed and had to kill (in Cynthia's case). I also prayed for Cynthia to come closer to my heart, for I wish... (*well, that will need further reflection*).

I also meditated thereupon that, as a soldier of the King, it was imperative we kept the King's interests, even if it included the interests of the natives unfairly ousted by an unregulated group of settlers (*especially as they were not properly British and it was obvious to us they did not wish to be*).

I finished and returned to the bed. Cynthia wore a white floral shift, as did I (but without the girly design) and she placed her arms around me for a loving embrace.

'Here,' I offered my lips and returned the favour. We kissed and kissed and soon, it got quite passionate.

I was very horny, as Cateliffe teased, and I thought it would be good to relieve myself within her, yet I decided not to because I did not wish for her to be inconvenienced. *Especially with this rebellion and all.*

'Do you have a stocking or something I can use to um.....,' I begged, gesturing toward my member.

'Ah, I can deal with that, Willec, sir.' She seemed so confident... as she... *augh!* I let out a scream as Cynthia climbed upon me to... to... *ahhh... ahhh...* I went for it and she treated me naturally.

'My dear, have you ever done this before?'

She stopped to answer, 'Only in my mind. I've dreamed of this moment for years, sir, for I shall suck the enormity of your valour.'

'Stop calling me, si--,' I gagged on my words, screamed again and in a matter of minutes, I got off on her floral bounty.

I laid flat, relieved of my duty. *Wow, what a girl. Phew!*

I came to my senses after a few minutes and confessed to Cynthia, 'This is the Age of Reason and as it stands to Reason, you should be with no one else but me.'

'You really know how to win a girl's heart, don't you?' She bent over me for a kiss.

A knock was at the door. Cynthia gasped and immediately removed herself from me. Cateliffe poked his head in, 'Willec, you sounded distressed?'

'Silly Cat, I sounded relieved!'

'Knew you were horny, sir.'

'Get out, we're fine!' I laughed and threw one of the odd cushions toward the door. Of course, Cateliffe got out of the way, missing the intended target... *damn!*

'Goodnight, Willec, pleasant dreams,' he called, as he and Nay-Smith giggled their heads off like schoolboys.

I turned to Cynthia, 'Now, you young lady, off to bed with you.'

'Will you be joining me? Remove your shift.'

'Remove yours first, ol' girl.'

She did. *Wow again.* I duly removed mine and we snuggled under the covers, sniggering ourselves into an enlightened sleep.

Yet, inevitably, she had to have the last word, 'I wish to engage you with the promise of my hearth.'

'We'll engage hearths tomorrow morning, do go to sleep.'

It had been the most restful sleep I've had since leaving Totterningstate.

Morning came with its pretty vengeance, removing the dark path that surrounded the land and revealing to all of what happened the previous night. Cynthia and I spent some time chatting before we got up and shared concerns about conversion, possible name change, finding her adoption papers (in order to have them legally rescinded), information on her natural father, (if any) and to send some of our men to ask around for further information regarding the Havènots that can be useful to the British cause.

After dressing, Cynthia was in the kitchen cooking, breaking from the dietary tradition to serve us a proper, hearty meal. There was enough food to muck around with for the purpose and, I dare say. she was a pretty good cook, too.

After gathering last minute items, including some jewellery inherited from her late mother, Cynthia and my lot met up with Crazypaws, who had our horses for our upcoming journey back to the barracks near the city. I thanked him for everything and he reciprocated. He was most appreciative that he did get his land back. The Catatoahs were not ones to hang about and already, the area we'd torched had been cleared away and revamped.

There was room for a tee-pee and a small campground to use as a base, while they figure out what to do with the homes and contents therein. Cynthia suggested to give them to the poor, as there was plenty of them round the area, and to pawn the more expensive items. The proceeds could go to the Indians as well as to help the British cause. The Chief agreed and had his people sort things out. We wished each other luck and hoped the area will be enjoyed for many years to come.

Crazypaws did not hesitate in his resettlement plans. In fact, he even decided to change the name of the area. He had the Scatsville sign removed and renamed the place Catskills, as his people, the Catatoahs were highly skilled for the land.

We left them to their deeds and made our way back to New York.

* * * * * *

'I see you have brought with you a souvenir from your little excursion,' Wolfe-Harris said, approaching me.

'Ha-ha,' I called out, 'Major General, how good it is to see you. Let me introduce you to Cynthia.'

'Hello, sir. Major General, wow!' She had a funny way of self-expressiveness.

'Never met one, had ye?'

'Nay, never,' she mimicked his tone.

The Major-General laughed, then got serious, 'You're the Havènot, girl, aren't you?'

She sighed, hoping he did not think less of her if she admitted to the same, 'Yes, I am, but I no longer wish to be. Could this be remedied? I mean, I've no ties nor family anymore. I am free.'

Free as a bird to marry me, I schemed to myself... *sorry Daff.*

'Indeed, you are free. Intelligence has told me of your exploits up there. Very impressive,' he turned to me, 'Willec?'

'Yes, Major General?'

'We need to talk. Have you received further intelligence about the grandfather and his doings?'

'Yes, Crazypaws informed me there was a congress in Philadelphia he was attending and said that they were thinking big.'

'Uh-oh, that confirms there *is* something going on. We were told about secret meetings in the State House. If this rebellion carries on, then whatever they are planning will be catastrophic. We cannot have that. We've got to get down there, post-haste.'

'Right,' I made a suggestion, 'We need remain here in barracks for now, as we have to deal with Cynthia's bits.'

'Oh?' Wolfe-Harris looked concerned.

'Well, it is like this,' I began to whisper her concerns we discussed to the Major-General.

'This sounds serious. She is really willing to change her entire life for our sake, records and all?'

'Yes and I want to make it so she is clean, with no connexions to sedition.'

'I'll send a detachment southward to see what's doing there, and in the mean whilst, make the girl more comfortable,' he winked at me.

'Yes, sir,' I saluted as he walked off.

Cynthia and I met up and we began to make plans for the future. Firstly, we needed some money, so she pawned all her mother's old jewellery previously packed. There was a necklace or two she wanted to keep, but the rings did not fit her and some of the brooches were very big for someone Cynthia's size. We received a very nice sum for the lot and I used some of the funds to buy her an engagement ring. I proposed to her there and then, casting my fate and all else to the sea. She accepted and was most happy to be an asset to myself. *She was even willing to assist our Cause to end this horrid rebellion.*

Then, she knew she had to change her surname and rid herself of the adoption to remove the stigma of her previous family. For the new name, we agreed on Haven. Cynthia Haven. Yes, that will work. We went to the courthouse and spoke to the clerk and judge. It was a slow day and we spent a good amount of time there. Once the filed adoption papers were produced, we requested them to be revoked immediately and preferably destroyed (so the adoption did not take place, at least on record). The judge was fair and knew of the Havènots and their way with Cynthia. *There was not a day they visited when they did not make a nuisance of themselves in front of the city's vast community*, he remembered. He agreed to the adoption revocation and the name change. We were also able to acquire her birth certificate, proving the old name of Silardicus (though a subsequent copy had reflected the adoption). Everything seemed to be in order, and I paid him some shillings for his trouble. The judge was on our side anyway, so it was just as kindly.

Cateliffe was appointed the task of finding out about Cynthia's natural father and asked around the community. It turned out that her father was named Joseph Silardicus and that it was confirmed the Havènots gave him an ultimatum (to which he refused), then cast him out. He lived on the streets of New York for years and never made it back to his native Italy. He came over for a new life and a hopeful bride, but he picked the wrong person, resulting in a child (Cynthia) being born. Just after being given the ultimatum, he had Cynthia baptised in a Roman Catholic church. The record had perished in an accidental fire, but the priest was tracked down and willing to sign a notification of certainty that Cynthia (under the name Silardicus), was indeed a baptised Christian.

However, as Cynthia grew up as a non-Christian, she wanted to have the baptism done anyway. The next day, Cateliffe, Nay-Smith, Cynthia and I went to an Anglican church to see to her entry into our faith. We explained the situation to the Rev Jonas Hathaway and he stated Cynthia was already a Christian. I asked him how that could be. He stated that if Cynthia had not be initiated into the other faith formally (which she was not, because she was *assumed* into it), her earlier baptism was very valid indeed. I produced the priest's statement regarding the early deed and Rev Hathaway said this was enough to prove she was part of Christendom already (and had been all along). The Reverend suggested she may renew her Christian vows, if that would make it any better for her. We both agreed and it was done.

During our stay in New York, I felt it would be best to break the tie legally from that family. I also felt strongly for Cynthia and wanted *her* (instead of Daff) to be my bride. On another visit to the same church, I asked the good Rev Hathaway if he could officiate our wedding. He heartily agreed, and, with good friends and some members of the companies still stationed in New York, Cynthia and I had taken the lifetime plunge into marriage.

The ceremony was short and sweet and Cynthia never looked sweeter than in a makeshift gown that was loaned by one of the officer's wives. The proper rings were arranged by Wolfe-Harris, as a favour to me and as an incentive to Cynthia in helping us out. *Don't worry, they will be put to good use.* He even gave Cynthia away, as she took her place beside me.

Rev Hathaway read out the service; I, awaiting the best bit, held onto Cynthia's hand, thinking, *this is my prize, this is my love.* Again, I thought, *sorry, Daff.*

The vows were taken. 'Do you, William Alexander Woodes-Hastings, take Cynthia Haven to be your lawfully wedded wife...?'

I wanted to climb to the moon. 'Yes, I do.'

The Rev turned to Cynthia to ask, 'Do you, Cynthia Haven, take William Alexander Woodes-Hastings to your lawfully wedded husband?'

'I do, I do, I DO!' she exclaimed proudly.

The rings were blessed and soon, the vows were sealed onto our fingers (so to speak). The service was shortly over... and I wholeheartedly rejoiced. Later, there was a celebration in the barracks and I, unceremoniously, was stripped bare, and thrown into a ready made bath tin, filled with champagne. The boys would have done Cynthia in too, but the bath was too small. It was fine, as I enjoyed their little gag.

* * * * *

Now, our attention was directed toward Cynthia's grandfather and his involvement with the Congress in Philadelphia. Half our regiment went south, the rest remained in New York. I accompanied various fellow soldiers, including Nay-Smith, Cateliffe and my new wife, Cynthia.

Our group, with a train of supplies, took horse and rode south. Cynthia was not used to riding, but she accepted it and made her way with us. To make it more certain for her, I allowed her to ride with me on the same horse.

It took a good many days for the trip and there were Loyalists about, willing to help us, sometimes with bed, food and/or relevant information. My love for Cynthia grew more as we journeyed on and further commenced our relations together.

I still did not want for her to become engrossed yet, out of consideration and convenience. She did not mind and thought our Cause was more important at this time than starting a family. *We could do that in England.* I loved the sweet child, and despite her being half my age, she was good enough for me. *If only my family could see me now...* despite their intentions for me to marry Daffnette. I dismissed the roaming thoughts, for they did not matter. I was content as a pie and I drove on, awaiting to finally break the Congress.

Chapter VIII

Our way to Philadelphia did not go unnoticed by the Rebels. *Sigh, they've got eyes and ears coming out of their arses!* A Rebel detachment, led by Captain Marlowe Unger-Miles (informally known to us as 'Hungry Miles' due to his never ending gluttony) had waited patiently for several days. Their spies knew we were marching forth... *yet we did not expect to go into battle.*

It was early July and the sunbeams were penetrating like lasers into our bright red uniforms. Cynthia needed more drinking than ever and we so tried to help. We stopped again for a rest before making the final push toward our goal. The foliage around us lay hushed and I looked around me ever so carefully. I wondered if those men realised we had a lady in our midst. Would they fire upon us if they did? Would they outwardly *intend* to kill her? I could not let the thought of losing Cynthia colour my attachment of the situation. Luckily, some Loyalists who helped us along had joined into our fold. We also had an attachment of Dragoons, led by a fellow called Tarleton, kindly sent to us from on high, *just in case.*

Suddenly, a shot rang forth as my men afoot sprang into action. The Rebels came after us like wildfire which had spread rather rapidly and several of our men were down in a flash. Martynne, Robshaw, Squires, Moss, Daniels, and Diarmud, to name but a few, were among the fatalities. Ah, Buckingham had a go at the rebel Captain and hit him fatally, point blank. *Good lad, all the training went to good use.* Tarleton rallied round to protect my wife, whilst I got off my horse to dispatch a few more of the enemy. A bullet had found my left shoulder, as I fell unto the ground.

Cateliffe yelled out and raced to my rescue, duly removing me away from the battle (*actually, I saw it as an unplanned ambush*).

'Christ, where is Cynthia?' I was livid with fear.

'Tarleton's got her with his men, and she is at the moment well guarded.'

I didn't like the sound of that, but I accepted my friend's word.

'Don't worry, Willec, she will be treated well. After all, she is on *our* side.'

'Yes... yes, Cateliffe, help me bandage this.' I dismissed the small talk, needing to be mended.

'With pleasure, sir.'

Cateliffe found some odd uniform material, taken from one of the dead, used it as a gauze to patch up the indiscretion put upon me.

I asked, 'Where are the others?'

'Heading after the rebels to finish them off... heading toward Lorne Bridge.'

'I see,' I contemplated. Lorne Bridge... *The Battle of Lorne Bridge. What cunning bastards.*

A short time later, Tarleton arrived with some personal goods.

'Colonel Woodes-Hastings, sir,' he announced.

'Yes?'

'Your wife. Unharmed and not worse for wear. I had to control her cos she wanted in on this too and tried to grab one of my men's sabres to involve herself in the melee. Silly girl needs teaching and practise. I cannot have an untrained person amongst us.'

'Points for effort, eh, Cynthia?' I winked at her.

Cynthia looked at me and Tarleton and, with cheek, stuck her tongue out and enquired brashly, 'Where the fuck is this congress thing?'

'A girl after my own heart,' Tarleton complimented her with a smile, 'I'll go see about any more fuss; you two should get a move on and take whatever you can with you.'

'Thank you, Ban, really,' I nearly cried.

He put his hand on my other shoulder, 'No problem, Willec. I do hope we meet again... it was a good volley we had today.'

'Agreed. I just wish it did not come with losses.'

'Never mind. Be seeing you,' he called out, as he mounted his horse, and rode off.

Nay-Smith came by, and felt like a wet dishcloth, exhaling, 'I think we've routed them. Whatever's left of them are on the retreat.'

Good, I figured that would happen. I mean, us British versus the scum of society? *Oh, come on!*

Nay-Smith looked at my shoulder, 'You've been wounded.'

'Really, sir, I had not noticed,' I stated sarcastically, as the wound continued to weep through the makeshift cloth.

Sergeant Clarence came along to gather up salvageable bits and bobs from the dead. Their uniforms, if reasonably intact, were removed from the body, and other effects, such as weaponry, were saved for future use.

The red coats would come in handy, as they always damage when worn, and bits or the whole could replace the lesser. Clarence was good like that... always reusing and refitting. Sometimes, our supplies lasted longer for this.

As the chaos ebbed away, some of our surviving men made up graves to bury our dead, and others had reassembled and we were on the march once again. We were unsure if there were any survivors in the rebel side, but none returned to give us bother.

I made way to my horse and tried to mount. *Damn, my shoulder.* Like hell, I struggled. Nay-Smith saw me and ran over to assist. He lifted me as best he could, (for I was not a lightweight), unto the beast. He helped Cynthia, too, as she resumed her place with me.

'I trust my kit is intact,' she hoped.

'I will see what we have remaining and inform you,' Nay-Smith offered.

'Shit, Willec, if those rebels fucked with my stuff, especially the paperwork...' Cynthia was most adamant.

'Do not worry. If anything, we can obtain new copies, buy new clothes, etc. If not, fuck 'em. You will no longer be here soon anyway, so for now, on to task.' I did not want her to give up hope, but I needed to toughen up her attitude toward the personal.

She gave me a kiss, which confirmed her understanding.

We rode on. *Clip-clop, clip-clop.*

* * * * * *

A day or two later, we finally arrived unmolested in Philadelphia. This city was no different to New York. *In fact, to me, they were all the same, for all I cared!* Some passers by were expecting our presence, however, some were disheartened.

The State House was not far and some of our group left Lorne Bridge earlier, like Tarleton's men, to secure those inside (in case any escapees came into view).

There was a crowd amongst us and things were getting jittery. I was still in shock from my wound and Cynthia felt an eager fatigue upon her. We had many men with us still, thank God, so we were happily well in numbers.

Tarleton, by now, had lay guard at the State House doors, with Rawdon and Simcoe and their respective companies, taking stand 'round the side arches of the building. The blockade was complete. Our men on horses dismounted, the foot soldiers climbed the stairs leading to the main chambers and this time, I would allow Cynthia to have the final say here.

We rushed into the building, entering the meeting room and the delegates were caught, point-black, with typical hang-dog looks on their faces. Some were determined, others knew their game was up. *I mean, what were they trying to prove anyway? To play government? Ha-ha... we knew better.* These men, with the finest colonial minds a land could offer, belonged behind a gavel or a market stall. I could not stop musing over these colonials... *they were so funny, they would make for great comedy in theatres back home... ah, wait a minute...*

However, Cynthia was not amused and she unabashedly burst into the room, where the delegates presided.

'There they are,' she proudly proclaimed, her grandfather amongst them.

She ran up to the high dais of the room and, despite her short stature (she was only just 5 feet, at least in her shoes), she snatched the crudely written piece of paper which the fellows herein were debating.

They looked at her with shocked countenances; their plans becoming undone by a wee slip of a girl. For the majority of her lifetime, she was underestimated by so many and now she was here to reclaim her moment of recompense... her moment of glory (*and ours, too*).

'Here. The document we've all been waiting for. Read it up, boys and enjoy the eloquence of the treason here printed against us. Independence!' She spat out the word as if it were a curse. The word blew our minds, as we took stock of the seriousness of this consideration.

My fellow officers and I had perused the document, to our disgust, and I had folded it up and placed it in my red uniform overcoat.

In the meantime, she eyed up every man in the room, including her grandfather and demanded redress for the grief many had caused her (*not that there were many within the stateroom, but they were intended targets, nevertheless*).

'These are the instruments which bore me nothing but grief. I am not surprised Grandfather was involved. He tried to be a father to me... when the family had cruelly cast out my natural father for NO GOOD REASON other than a clash of background. My father died on the streets of New York because of them,' she pointed at the grandfather, *bearing the responsibility upon him and his whole family.*

The grandfather was reserved for some real hostility, as Cynthia's anger was directed toward him....

'And YOU are directly responsible, chasing my father away and casting him out into the cold street. He was an innocent, who did nothing to you... whose only crime was marrying your daughter.'

The grandfather spoke, 'The casting out was my wife's idea. I am really sorry. Are you really allied to this treachery against us?'

'Your wife was more treacherous than the WHOLE British army combined!' Cynthia shouted, 'You lot had NO RIGHT to do what you did to him and tear me away from a goodly heritage.'

The grandfather looked remorseful, making feeble excuses. 'It was not my fault. We did not know what else to do.'

Cynthia fumed violently at this when Cateliffe volunteered, 'Do you know what happened to your family, Mr Havènot?'

'No, I do not. How would I know, when I am here.'

I cleared my throat to reveal, 'There was a raid on the community in Scatsville by the Indians. Everyone in the town who were present in the temple were all killed in a fire there.'

'There was a fire?' Mr Havènot was astounded. 'My wife... ?'

'Yes,' Cateliffe confirmed.

'But Cynthia is alive. How can this be?'

'The British rescued me from your evil community,' Cynthia screamed, 'How DARE you consider me part of a group of

TRAITORS.' She spat out the final word; again, like a curse. *God, she's good.*

She continued the rant, 'And for what? To start anew when one is ill prepared for it? To deny my British identity just cos you do not want to pay your taxes?! Your infighting, endless debating, the spying and the irresponsibility of founding a new nation, so what of it? You couldn't found a nation if it were left on your doorstep of a hospital! How dare you, to take away a King, who may be far away and your representation in his government *may* be in question. Yet, he is in full faculty of his subjects. What's more, the King is British, not German. God, you cannot even get that right! His family may be of German background, but he himself was born and raised in England....London, in fact. Your flaming ignorance of everything beyond your shores is astonishing. The King would be most jubilant if he were here, right now, with me... to find everybody in one place, in one's own order, creating disorder amongst the many classes of British colonial society. He would be so delighted to have all you provocateurs gathered in one place, ripe for arrest. *I bet he would not hesitate to throw a grenade at you and blow this place up!'*

I was getting uncomfortable with what the dear lass was saying... true, she showed loyalty, but my God, I did not think she had it in for everyone.

She carried on, nonetheless, 'You lot, you snakes in the glass of good wine... you think you could take away a system that worked since these shores were populated. You think you could take away the dignity of a far away nation that settled here, made laws and culture... a lifestyle?? You think you could create your *own* laws and culture? You don't have any and you will only copy ours. **I WILL TAKE BACK WHAT IS MY RIGHT AS A BRITISH SUBJECT** and will flatly refuse to become an 'American citizen'. The latter is more repulsive to me than vomiting out a slug.'

There was a heavily pregnant pause (which overrode the potential birth of a nation), when one of the delegates rose to speak. I was surprised it was not the Grandfather, as I figured her aggrieved state was due to family matters. I guessed wrong.

'So what do you intend to do with us, now you have your evidence of our 'so-called' treason. Please enlighten us... what are you going to do, throw a tea party?'

It was John Adams who spoke. He thought he could have another go at us, considering his cousin, Samuel, was a real buggernaut in our struggle to keep the colonies. He and a few others up in Boston started this shit in the first place... *now, it was payback time.*

There was another pause... did my good lady take more than she bargained for? I noticed her heckles rose to the fore, as I realised I thought too soon.

'You will all be carted off to London to be put on His Majesty's Display.'

'Ma'am, if I may,' another delegate, Ben Franklin, piped up, 'I have heard of His Majesty's Pleasure, which would make a fitting end to us all, if you do not intend to kill us. What do you mean by His Majesty's Display?'

'It is for me to know and for you to find out after a several month journey on a wobbly ship back to England. Hurrah!' She laughed after the retort. *I could no longer take the heat of her anguish.*

'Enough now, Cynthia, enough,' I demanded, pulling her aside, 'Your fifteen minutes are up. Let us take leave.'

We left the room to cool off, or at least, to let my love do so.

A murmur arose, as the baffled delegates awaited our decision against them... *ha-ha, let them wait!*

Tarleton waited outside the door where Cynthia was left to take a breather.

'I heard what you said in there. I am quite proud of you. I could not put it better myself,' he commended.

'You do not know how many years of stored ammunition THAT produced.'

'I can believe it; a real magazine explosion,' he sighed, 'You alright?'

'Not really, to tell the truth. That took a lot out of me,' she exhaled.

'I think it would have done so with me as well.'

'I'm going back in,' I said to her, giving her a tender kiss. I turned to Tarleton, 'Look after her for me for a moment, please.'

Tarleton nodded, 'We'll be here.'

'God, you are not going back in there, Willec.' *Cynthia was scared for me.*

'Do not concern yourself. I will be with you shortly,' I reassured her.

I returned to the room and, in my Britannical best, announced, 'By His Majesty King George III, of which you are all his subjects, I am placing you under arrest for Defying His Majesty's Rule by Open Rebellion and Treasonous Meetings, and you are, as the good lady stated, to return to England, on the aforesaid wobbly ship. Your fate will be determined in London, on the King's terms, and at the King's pleasure. Mr Havènot will be detained here for further investigation. Take them away!'

I, too, needed a break... *I think we all did.*

My men bundled the group up and led them unceremoniously out of the state house to ride them out to the harbour for their coming journey. As I watched the procedure, I reread the colonial document Cynthia had taken from the hopeful delegates. *Whoa, she was right.* My early perusal did not catch the drift (for we all were carried away by the lady's harried speech). It was some form of declaration of independence, *an early draft, perhaps.* Ummm... one dares to imagine what oddities this would create if *this* got out. *Oh dear!*

This capture would bring glorious news for our King. He would be over the moon to see the rebellion crushed and his colonies remain intact. We had Cynthia to thank for all this. The conflict was over... for *them.* I laughed quietly and walked out of the hall to find Cynthia.

Chapter IX

We remained in Philadelphia until a galley ship, the HMS *Going Places*, returned to the colonies from England. More of the King's troops were to be stationed here, as in all port cities, to keep the order and to weed out the troublemakers. Overall, our little stint at the State House went swimmingly, yet it will take time for those feeling otherwise to warm to our presence. Still, the main group of delegates were set to be shipped back home, where the King will deal with them. Cynthia's grandfather was detained for a different purpose. We had not determined what his fate would be and we relied on Cynthia to fill us in on any details to assist with our enquiry.

There was a barracks available, which allowed us to repose and compose our order. Some of our lot went on policing duties and did their rounds throughout the City to be certain peace was kept (*and kept quiet, preferably*). I was told to stay with Cynthia and find out more about Mr Havènot. It was not long before she decided to share some information with us about him and the family. It did not take much time to question her, which I took charge of.

'They tried to convince me that I was not a British subject, despite these being *your* colonies. They encouraged me to believe in an independent America and to be an American. When I asked them about myself (being independent, as I am of age), they dismissed the notion and kept banging on about their religion and that I was forever part of it. There was nothing I could do to remedy that condition.'

I had to confirm, 'So they used religion in their ideological warfare against you?'

'Yes. It was getting far too personal. Grandfather was always out and about, giving money to the Revolutionary cause, earning a fair bit in business and whatever.'

'So he was rallying sedition?'

'Looks like it.'

Heaven, I never thought. I knew she did not think of subversion against us, *but the cowardice and rebellion of her family....*

'About your natural father, what happened to him (for the record)?'

'He was given an ultimatum, to which he refused, and was chased off. My mother was in her family's custody and care until she died. Before so doing, they had her divorce my father and have hers and my name legally changed before they adopted me and took over my life.'

'Why was your mother in her family's custody?'

'She was epileptic and they felt she was not of sound mind and they assumed I was equally unbalanced, just because I was her daughter.'

'That is not sound logic. You are a very capable woman, Cynthia Woodes-Hastings,' I affirmed to her. It was so satisfying to be able to call my love by her newly married name. *Ah, life was so good to me.*

'I appreciate your kindness, sir.'

'You stop calling me sir, or I'll belt ya,' I teased, 'You are my wife, not my subordinate.'

'Sometimes women are subordinate to men.'

'Not in MY order!' Now, it was time for her to see *my* side of familial rebelliousness.

She was taken aback by my comment and replied, 'You are too generous to me and I hope you do not think ill of me because I came from such a pack of wolves.'

'It is you who are being too generous. I can see what they did to you... they tried to discredit you, and disregard you to their oblivion. Well, we show'd them, eh?'

We had a laugh together and remembered Crazypaws and his tribesmen. I heard the land was successfully resettled and the houses were kept for the poor white folk in the area who were ousted by the community we had cleared off. The Chief did not care to live as the whites did. He was more than happy to let them stay on the property (within reason) and carry on camping on the clear bits of land that was his and his ancestor's before him. I really missed him and hoped for the best for his people.

I took note of all that Cynthia told me and reported it to my superior officer, Wolfe-Harris. It was not long before an execution order was made out and dispatched quickly, an example to be made of him for treason. The other delegates whom we arrested would be taken into further custody aboard the ship and kept in the hold.

Shortly afterwards, Cateliffe came by, a bag brimming with the salvaged paperwork (regarding Cynthia) from the previous meeting with the rebels.

'I think, Mrs Woodes-Hastings, you should have a look at all this,' he said, unloading it unto a table in the room, 'Now that you have settled with us, you need to see it.'

The paperwork was in a pile that Cynthia had carefully checked with great interest. She found the documents regarding birth, baptism, renouncement of adoption, change of name and the most important of all, our marriage certificate.

'Thank you,' she said, kissing Cateliffe.

'That was refreshing,' he said upon departure from the room.

'Go on,' I jested at him.

* * * * * *

The HMS *Going Places* was ready to depart for England. We boarded the ship with our regiment, and my dear wife, Cynthia. I was so happy to see she was coming with us on this voyage.

A midshipman, Edfriar, made rounds and checked the passenger lists. He turned to me, 'Colonel and Mrs Woodes-Hastings?'

'Yes, that is right,' I asserted.

'Welcome aboard,' he said, aiming at the wife.

'Much obliged,' she noted.

We went on board with some kit, as Cynthia gave away most of her things which she brought from her home, as well as selling the more expensive bits. *She really wanted a break from the past, and it showed.*

Another crewman had shown us to our cabin. It was white walled, airy, with lots of light coming in through both windows at each end. There was a four poster double bed of dark wood, a desk and chair, a commode, a dresser... *wait a moment, this looks like the...* I turned around to see my in-law, Greyrivers.

'Willec, it had been too long,' he said.

'Pomphrey,' I acknowledged.

We hugged for an instant as I gazed upon him. A man just about six foot, slender in build, smart naval uniform identifying him as the Captain (*if one knew where to look*) and a kind face with sparkling hazel eyes, firm nose, round chin.

'Hello, what do we have here?' Greyrivers was quite observant when he spotted Cynthia next to me.

'This is my wife, Cynthia,' I introduced to him.

'The Havènot girl?' Greyrivers was partly privy to the mission. He was to provide the departing ship to leave these contestable colonies.

I whispered in his ear, 'She no longer goes under that name. In fact, we changed it before I married her. *She is a Woodes-Hastings, now.*'

'Pardon my ignorance, Colonel, and do forgive me. I was aware there was a girl involved, but I did not expect you to marry her...,' Greyrivers looked at me, 'Um... Willec, we need to talk.'

'And talk we shall, 'twill be a two month journey, give or take a week,' I smirked.

'As you can guess, these are the Captain's quarters, which you can use for yourselves. I am sure it will be adequate for you and your missus. I know the ins and outs of the ship to find an alternative arrangement.'

'Sure thing,' Cynthia chimed, 'I love it already. Thank you very much.' She kissed Greyrivers.

'Splendid, I salute you, the newest member of the Woodes-Hastings clan, by marriage.'

I whispered in her ear that Greyrivers was an in-law in our family, too.

'But, you are still a Greyrivers,' she added.

'Ah, I am not of the sex which kindly gives in to one's partner in order to commence change.'

Ha-ha, give it a rest, Greyrivers!

'I need to return to deck. Mr Slaiter will see to your needs in the meantime. See you later.' Greyrivers left the room.

'Cheers,' I called out.

My in-law turned round, nodded with a salute.

I got into the chair and fumbled for my pipe.

'Ah, you smoke,' she observed.

I took a quick puff and said, 'Yes, but casually. It is nought a huge habit. Just a passing vice. You got any?'

'Any what, sir?'

Oh God, she needn't still call me 'sir', for she was now my wife and had to get used to the fact. This may take awhile... *what will I ever do with her?*

I asked her again, 'Got any vices?'

'Oh, I am sorry, I thought you wanted me to hand you some tobacco.'

Not that she had any...

'Sorry, it would be something I would ask of my men. I did not think you were in the habit.'

'Oh I see,' Cynthia went to the bed's edge to sit down. The window was open and let in a fair breeze. It was most beautiful outside and we both settled in well.

We were about to raise anchor when suddenly, there was a commotion at the quay. A black fellow, (or may I say, a runaway slave) was running toward our ship, trying to board her.

'Hey, hey, hey, where do you think you're going?' Mr Slaiter stopped the desperate fellow.

'Not back there, sah,' the runaway panted, 'I want out!'

'Not for the likes of you. You don't even have a ticket for passage.'

'I'll work for my passage, sah.'

'What is your name boy?'

'Luthar Amos, formerly Yokebowan.'

'I do not need to know your African affiliation. You are a lucky one today, Mr Amos. We could use an extra hand here. We want to return to England with a smooth passage. You think you can handle that? Once we do get to England, you have a choice to remain on board as a crewman (if you do well), or you can be sold on. Your choice.'

'No, massa, I go with you. No bring back to colony.'

'Why? Where did you come from?' Slaiter was getting suspicious.

'Mandrake Grove, Terraminde County is all I know. It is in southern area.'

Slaiter reflected, 'Yeah, it is a horrible place. Come on board, Mr Amos, we're weighing anchor.'

'Yassah,' Mr Amos agreed, already on deck.

'Now you report to crewman Moore and he will show you the ropes.'

Mr Amos saluted and went about his duties. The ship had left port by now and we were heading out to the open sea. I witnessed the exchange and had a brutally silly idea.

'Mr Slaiter,' I called.

'Yes, Colonel?'

'That slave you brought aboard, um,' I had to think fast, 'What would it take to take him off your hands by our journey's end?'

'Oh, when we return to England, sir?'

'Yes...'

'Well, I was hoping to use him aboard the ship in future.'

Too bad. I had a better solution. 'I have a slave back home in Totteringstate called Fantasie and we need a companion for her. That fellow would be a perfect match for her and he can work on our pig farms.'

'You're the fabled Woodes-Hastings of Totteringstate?'

I nodded.

Mr Slaiter looked at me. 'Are you trying to match up niggers, sir?'

I had to admit to a slight giggle, as I did not realise my intention would be a statement of amusement to another. *I meant it to be beneficial.* 'What of it? They breed, don't they?'

'Don't we all?' Mr Slaiter let go a laugh, 'There would be more for your plantation.'

'In England, we have estates, not plantations,' I snootily replied (*actually, in fun*).

'Right. Name your price.'

'You keep him 'til we get to England; I will give you £12 for Mr Amos.'

'Twelve pounds?'

'Directly to you, Mr Slaiter,' I assured, walking with him towards my cabin.

'Twelve pounds it is, then,' he spit in his hand, as did I, and we shook on it. Our bargain was complete.

'I've got to get back. See you later,' Mr Slaiter walked away toward his crewman and began shouting orders at them.

I turned away, highly amazed at what I'd just done, and returned to the cabin.

Cynthia was thumbing through one of the books the Captain had on the shelf. The door was open and I believe she was privy to my conversation with Mr Slaiter.

'Hello, my dear, what are you reading?'

She turned to me and showed me. It was a book about naval history. She looked out the window, 'Are you picking up more of them?'

I stood aghast, 'Whatever do you mean, love?'

'I heard what you did. You bought a slave, rescuing him, perhaps. You offered good money for him.'

'Ah, so I had. I have a slave girl back home at Totteringstate who is in need of companionship, as do you...,' I trailed off for a bit, 'You upset?'

'Nah, I just thought it was out of character to buy a slave like that on the fly. I thought you were a common soldier, a normal, typical Englishman, or whatever you are, not someone who would befriend Indians, rescue a girl from a non-Christian community and buying a slave, only to hook him up with one of your own. It seems there is something really special about you. You are not like the others. It's as if you want to save the world or something.'

Me, a saviour? She does have a way with words.

'Soldiers are supposed to save the world, as it were... that is why we fight; to keep order of things, to establish peace. It is only due to people like your grandfather who make us fight and show our bayonets to everyone.'

Cynthia snapped, 'Don't blame me, just cos my family was seditious and believed in the wrong side!'

'No, my dear,' I cooed, 'I am not blaming you,' I reinforced my love with a hug, 'I am sorry I mentioned him.'

'That is fine,' she forgave, 'It is apparent we have much to discuss.'

'We've got this journey together and will discuss any matter you care to. Once we finish, we will put it behind us and move on. Agreed?'

'I would like that, yes,' she stated, 'I really do not want my past to be mentioned in better circles, now that I am your wife. It is such a noxious offence to me that it would embarrass me to no end. It is not my fault they wanted me to be something I wasn't and the way I was *treated* by them was inexcusable.'

'Inexcusable in many farther circles, I might add,' I confirmed, 'I will practise discretion if your bits come up in conversation.'

'So you are not offended by my person?'

'Why should I be offended? You are a lovely creature and by God, I am glad to have you as family. Actually, if it weren't for your family's trespasses against you, you would not be in the state of mind you are currently in, that is to say, loyal to our Cause.' *She is so insecure.*

'You are right. The British Empire must not fail.'

Such devotion was rare. *I wondered how much of the abuse she suffered from them made her think in such a manner.*

It was a good clear day and the waters beneath were (so far) calm. I know these transatlantic journeys can be rough passage, and stormy seas can lie ahead. Yet, would the storms be from Neptune's offspring, or the little lady who made a pledge and gave up everything for me and the Cause?

Chapter X

A few days passed and Cynthia was getting restless and slightly bored on the ship. I was used to the lag, having done the *Atlantic cruise* once before. I coached Cynthia and tried to prepare her for this, but she still felt out of sorts. Out of my bounds, she took it upon herself to offer assistance aboard to Mr Slaiter, who was taken aback by her boldness.

'Can you climb rigging? You look young and healthy enough,' he offered.

'I'm scared of heights, sir.'

'Yeah, we'll leave that to the boys, shall we?' He let out a laugh.

'I can help scrub the deck.'

'You are too good to be a scrubber.'

'Well, I can work on a small area, everyday if you wish. It would give me something to do...'

Mr Slaiter interrupted, 'And my men less work.'

'I can work for an hour or so. Would that be sufficient?' Cynthia looked hopeful.

'I'll give you a go, for now. However, if the Colonel objects, let my men do the task.'

'Fine. I will do that,' she said.

'Here you are,' he said, giving her the implements to scrub her part of the deck with, 'You might want to change into something less tidy. We have stores in here,' he showed her some extra sailor's uniforms.

She changed her clothes into her 'working' gear and began her hour to *do her bit*.

I rested among my men, playing cards, smoking, drinking and whatever else we did the last time we rode on these hulking ships.

I walked upon the deck with Cateliffe, only to see my dearest love, an aristocrat by marriage, slogging it out in britches and loose fitting shirt, mopping the deck. It was most unseemly for the dear lady. I nearly had tears in my eyes.

'Willec, is that...?' Cateliffe was astounded.

'Yes, it is,' I confessed to him. I went over to Cynthia to find out what in blazes was going on with her.

'My love,' I said soothingly, touching the mop handle to get her attention, 'Who made you do this? Why are you slopping out?!'

'I did, Willec. I thought to help out for an hour a day, just to pass the time.'

I was a little miffed she chose to do labour when she could spend that sweet hour (*and, in fact, all day*) with me.

'In our home, you will not be expected to do daily chores. That is reserved for servants and/or slaves. You are a lady... *my lady*.'

'I see. I am used to doing this, and I wanted to help. Mr Slaiter said it would be alright to do so,' Cynthia insisted.

'Well, you carry on,' I relented, 'I will see you in an hour.'

I walked away to meet with Mr Slaiter and asked him, 'Did Cynthia really volunteer for this?'

'Ready and able as a seaman, sir,' he confirmed.

God, this menial work would be so demeaning for her.

'As long as it was her that suggested and offered,' I said.

'Colonel... Willec... I,' he was firm in tone, 'I've got a near full crew and that nigger we let aboard had filled the compliment. With Cynthia involved, wanting to join in, I'm not complaining. She is most enthusiastic.'

I thought about the confrontation at Lorne Bridge and how Tarleton noted her *enthusiasm* in wanting to fight alongside his troops against the rebels.

'But I am complaining.' I stood firm, too.

'It is up to her. Let her go on; she must be used to doing housework of some form.'

'Yes, and now she must get used to leisure, which is *our* way of life.'

'An hour should not be a problem, would it?'

'An hour it is. I will agree to it, for now.'

Mr Slaiter brought up the Amos fellow. 'What about the money for the slave?'

'He is yours until this passage is terminated, then he will go to me and I will pay you then.'

I went back to my place with Cateliffe and leaned on the side. I looked at my watch. It was another half hour to go. *Surely Cynthia could spend more productive time than this.*

Once the gruesome torment of waiting was done, I met up with my wife as she handed her cleaning gear to the sailor who would continue the job on another bit of the deck.

'Come here,' I beckoned her.

She came over to me and gave me a long kiss. 'Yes?'

'I want to talk to you.'

'About what?'

We walked over to our cabin quarters. On our way, I spotted Greyrivers waving hello to us. The wave was duly returned as we entered the cabin. Inside, Cynthia looked for something more feminine to wear, *at my insistence.*

'It is not like anyone will know. It is a ship, you know, relaxing,' she stated.

How naive thou art, my love.

'There are people aboard, everywhere, who can say things about you. If you carry on like this, you could be cruelly ridiculed... and with your past, it would cause further damage to my reputation, saying I married well-beneath me. Our family never had problems with marrying beneath them, as it did not really matter to us... if anyone said anything against us, we would scoff it off. Yet, you are giving, nay, *offering,* ammunition for ridicule. You do not need this.

'I appreciate your industry and I understand you grew up doing house chores, but now your life is different. You are my wife, a lady, my true love. Please do not give those who do not need to know about you anything for them to investigate. If you want to get past your former life, please do so.'

'I am used to it, I thought they could use some help.'

'Well, they do not. I spoke to Mr Slaiter myself.'

'Oh,' she looked regretful, possibly downcast.

'Look, I am not angry at what you've done. It is a kindness, but a kindness that could be taken advantage of by the other men, or misconstrued by my fellows. A pretty girl like you, married...,' I warned.

'It was only a chore to pass the time with. I do apologise if I caused a problem.'

I gave her a hug. 'You did not cause any problem or harm,' I soothed her, 'I guess choring is better than whoring. I will tell Mr Slaiter you will forfeit your hour to the crewmen.'

'Alright. I'm sorry,' she pouted, but thought better of it. If she is bored and does work, the men do not have work and if they are idle, who knows what could happen. The tightened and disciplined routine would be terribly compromised at a high cost... *and that is a cost I am not willing to pay.*

I hugged Cynthia and helped her remove the britches and shirt. She looked ravishing to me and I so, so wanted in... *in her.*

'Now that we're away from that land mass, I think you and I should commence relations,' I suggested.

'At last. It was nice what I did to you after that raid you planned.'

I looked upon that memory with titillating fondness and began removing my britches, waistcoat and shift. I realised it was nearly lunch, *but I was hungry for something else.*

We went under the bed covers and held one another tightly. I looked at her and gave her a lasting kiss, putting my tongue in her mouth, feeling the velvety smooth flesh against hers. Cynthia held me quite firmly, as I reciprocated her earlier pleasure upon me. I lowered myself as I rubbed her glory, and, in seeking out the oral party, the pleasant sensation of her natural flow broke its inner hold. She cried aloud, and *ah, at last,* I felt her lively simulation as I began the next phase of my plan. I mounted her, as I would my horse, and endeavoured to gain entry into her estate. I kissed her fine lips as I continued to swirl around her. Her enclosure was hell-bent on acquiring my attributes. There was no room for pride in a court room of tenderness, as we dreamed and drooled in our own landscape.

'You've aroused me whole. I... I cannot hold back any longer,' I exclaimed excitedly.

There was a tiny struggle in the roomful of eternity;
And it felt I had received a meat bundle from Dorset.
Her loins hath delicately encompass'd me,
As I paid her the honour of due release.

She declared, with volume, 'I felt the flesh of your specimen and I am besotted with the juices flowing from thee!'

Cynthia was the poetic one today. *Could it have been that hour without me?*

I had my way with her, and she with me, and we were both elated. We cleaned ourselves up and a knock was heard at the door. I went up to answer. Cateliffe, Nay-Smith and Buckingham stood there grinning like schoolboys on a jolly day out.

'Come in you lot, and don't you say anything,' I warned them.

'Willec, you cannot deny it; we know what happened here,' Cateliffe said, smiling.

'We wanted to see how you were getting on with your new girl,' Buckingham quipped, 'Daff may not be pleased.'

'I can now see why you did not turn up for lunch,' Nay-Smith started, 'You were sorely missed.'

Lunch. *Oh blast, I forgot.* Yet, was I hungry? *I think not.* As far as Daff was concerned... oh well, *what could I do?* I fell in love... me, a silly soldier of the King. One does not fall in love with the oddball colonist... *but that is the lot of a Woodes-Hastings.*

'Never mind Daffnette,' I crossly spoke to Buckingham, who poorly stifled a giggle which had the costume of full-blown laughter.

Cynthia turned around, and enquired, 'Who's Daffnette?'

'Eh, Cynthia?' I was caught out. *Oh Lord... what to do. We will need to talk soon about this.*

'Also, you got anything decent 'round here? Do you have anything to eat that doesn't crawl about or look at you whilst eating? I heard about these ships and the limited keep of stores,' she whinged.

It would be hard to find decent food for her by now... this little one needs something but may have to accept something less-than-par.

Cateliffe offered, 'I can weed out the movements and you can soak the rest up with rum, how does that sound?'

She made a face, 'It will have to do; nothing gross, now, you hear? At least I can lose some weight whilst on this crazy voyage.'

'But you look lovely,' Nay-Smith said.

"T'would be nothing gross, milady,' Cateliffe continuing to joke, 'But it cannot be as gross as what happened in this room, if I am guessing correctly.'

Our room of eternity needed no hosts. Buckingham howled.

'Shut up, Cat!' I shouted and threw the used linen, which hit its mark, straight at his face.

'Ugh,' he cried, and left the room with the rest of them. Cynthia continued to get dressed as did I, but without my red coat. I did not really need it aboard the ship and it was nice to do without it. It was more comfortable; we were not on duty anyway (*and it showed*).

* * * * * *

I spent time with the fair Cynthia for the rest of the journey. She relented with regards to deck duties, as I and my close friends in the company made use of the time together, getting to know her and where she gets her endless drives from. We included her in our card games and other frivolities we ourselves had indulged in aboard the ship. Although my friends were not privy to her entire ordeal, she gave enough information to make them most sympathetic to her.

It was why we were more than willing to assist her in her cause, as she was equally and duly willing to assist in ours. *I, however, was given the full regalia of detail, which made my bones shake.* From what I saw at the Havènot residence, it seemed plain, ordinary and average for a 'middling' family of her state (despite the showy decor and self-evident ambition). In reality, I wonder if an interview with the walls therein would give a much fuller story. She told me there were many arguments and not a day passed between those within the household in which a kind word was said to Cynthia.

I'm sure there *may* have been exceptions, but the overall synopsis of their *supposed* caring made Cynthia feel like she was prey to *their* whims and expectations, rather than the family letting her get on with her life and move on like the rest of us.

I gave Cynthia a hug as she revealed more to me.

'They even challenged my being a British subject, as I told you before. The ancestors a couple of generations back made certain of the severance of their own pasts. As a result, my maternal family's attitude and lifestyle depended on it. *Their lie depended on it.* They believed that once a Jew, always a Jew, and I found this difficult to stomach, especially since we found out otherwise.'

'Yes, my dear, we did... and you will not continue to believe their lies, then?'

'It is hard to let go of something so strongly ingrained.'

'You do not believe you are of them?'

'No, I do not. Yet, if one states that shit smells sweet, enough times, the stench will become like fragrance.'

'Well, with a stench like that, it seems that you can handle anything,' I encouraged.

'I am unsure of that, sir.'

'Now, what did I say?'

'About what?'

'Calling me *sir*,' I said primly.

'Oh, sorry, I keep forgetting... when one has been brought down so much, it begs belief that anything good can come of it.'

'I will let that go, for now. You must let go, too. Your personality has yet to fly and I am about to give it wings.'

I was kind like that, and carried on, 'You must think like a predator. You are no longer a victim, or prey, in this case. You can do it and I personally believe in you, my dear Cynthia. No matter what, I will always love and support you. In fact, though we are married, how would you like to have a vow renewal ceremony in England at Totteringstate, so our loved ones can see what I've brought home with me and to further declare my endeavours to you.'

'We were married in haste, I admit,' she agreed, 'I look forward to meeting your relatives.'

'I've a brother who can help us with this. His name is Lottie.'

'That's an odd name for a bloke.'

'His full name is Lancelot John. He is my twin.'

'Oh, there are two of you?'

'Yes, that is correct,' I smiled, 'He might be able to help you adapt to our ways. You have made your commitment to Christ, and he can give you further instruction and indoctrination in our church. Perhaps he can arrange your confirmation.'

'I trust it is similar to the one where I renewed by baptismal vows and we married in.'

'Similar... but you will be going to the heart of the English Church. With your spirit, you will be most welcome there. I trust you enjoy the traditional styles or would you want the more expressive outlook?'

'Expressive?'

'Yea, some churches broke away from the Church of England stating it was not enough of a Protestant church. Several people created offshoots like the Methodists, Presbyterians, Baptists, and the like.'

'I have seen buildings of that nature over the years passing through New York and travelling in the outer regions of the colony. I often wondered about them.'

'Well, you needn't. You will be made anew in England and your past will soon be quickly forgotten, *but it is up to you.*'

'I know, Willec.' She grabbed me for another supportive hug. I must admit, she was a much better option than Daffnette. *Heaven, what have I got myself into?*

I realised that conversation with Greyrivers will come sooner than thought.

Chapter XI

The weeks went by, sullenly, as the ship had been on a slow but smooth path back home. I relaxed on deck in one of the makeshift chairs reserved for officers, smoking my pipe. The crew had carried on with their duties, making certain our time aboard would be most swift, if possible. My wound was tended to regularly by the surgeon, thankfully healing nicely. Cynthia, finally, allowed herself to enjoy her newfound leisure and she played cards again with Cateliffe, Nay-Smith, Buckingham and occasionally myself (*when I was not in one of my more thoughtful moods*). The prisoners we transported below deck were reasonably looked after, though in confinement. I looked forward to seeing how their fates would play out in England.

I spotted Greyrivers walking on deck, doing his rounds. I called him over, and he brought over another chair next to mine.

Greyrivers began, 'So, how's it going for you, Willec?'

'Tough, I think,' I remarked, 'Cynthia's a due challenge for me.'

'Enthusiastic, I noticed. What happened to her?'

I explained a bit about the domineering rebel family and how she helped us in our Cause to retain the colonies. I durst not go into detail, as I sworn my confidential allegiance to Cynthia.

'Yet, she will adapt,' I replied.

'Guess so. Oh, I have news for you from Totteringstate.'

Uh-oh... Daffnette? Family? Oh my!

I looked at him directly in the eye, 'What news from our Totteringstate?'

'I received a letter from my wife dockside. Your father has died. Your brother conducted the funeral.'

His wife, of course, was my sister, Emmadayle. *I was sad to hear about Father*, yet, a more urgent matter took over.

'Pomphrey, what about Daff?' I was most eager to ask, as now that I've got Cynthia, there will be hell to pay if I do not find out about my former intended.

'It was discussed before your father's death and, as you were not present during this arrangement, Daff decided to go for your brother after all. She is still fond of you, however.'

'I am sure she is... I think Lottie is the better choice for her, as I've stated all along. I know she was most sweet to me and really thought I was for her.'

'I did not want to hide this from you, Willec. With Cynthia around Totteringstate, things may go tottering off between them.'

I did not think Daff would be cruel to Cynthia; my dearest wife had enough to bear for one. Daff was not that clever enough to make a scene or say wicked things to Cynthia, so I could not see why they would not get on.

'I appreciate you telling me.'

'No problem, Willec. I've got to head off now.'

'Thank you,' I said, as he walked away toward his first officer and had a chat.

I looked away toward the horizon, hoping we will reach England soon.

* * * * * *

After a further considerable few weeks, there was a shout 'LAND HO!'

The crew and officers scrambled on deck to find white cliffs in the distance. Cynthia and myself leant toward the side of the ship. We felt elated and thanked God for a (reasonably) safe journey. We could fully (and finally) put the shit behind us and look forward to happy lives ahead.

'See that, Cynthia,' I pointed outward, 'That is our home. England. Your life as an Englishwoman has begun.'

She pulled on her red skirt and adjusted her blue floral shift. 'So they were wrong.'

'Who?' *Ah*, I remembered. *That family!* 'Yes, quite. They were *wrong* in the most certain way possible.'

'At last,' she cried with elation and hugged me. I let off another smile and gave her a kiss.

As the shore drew nearer, we returned to our cabin and began to pack our things. Once our stuff was packed away and all looked good, I watched us dock at Sydmouth Harbour. I completed my business with Mr Slaiter, paying him the £12 with regard to taking charge of Mr Amos. I welcomed him into our fold.

'So you now own me, Massa?'

'Stop talking like you're from the South. You are now embarking on a new life, just like Cynthia. Do refer to me as Colonel or sir, please,' I suggested.

'Yes, sir. Thank you. You must be looking forward to going home.'

'I do look forward to our arrival,' I remarked back, with a cool demeanour.

We filed out of the ship, once moored, and I went to my friends to bid them farewell.

'Guess we won't be seeing you for awhile,' Cateliffe said.

'You will see us soon enough,' I stated in hope.

'We'd been through a lot together,' Buckingham reflected, 'I, for one, will miss you.'

I embraced him, 'And I, you.'

'Good luck with Cynthia,' Nay-Smith wished us well, 'Let us know when your marital renewal takes place. I do not want to miss that.'

'You were present at our wedding in New York.'

Nay-Smith laughed. *I knew what he meant.* I looked at Cynthia and kissed her.

She turned to my friends, 'Thank you. Thank you for all your help.'

'One good turn deserves another,' Cateliffe answered, 'You helped us.'

'Yes, that she did,' Buckingham shook Cynthia's hand and kissed it.

She blushed merrily as we parted company. Out of the corner of my eye, I saw Mr Slaiter removing the prisoners for their one way trip to the Tower.

I harrumphed to myself and pressed on, holding Cynthia by the hand. Mr Amos, meanwhile, came in very useful as a baggage handler.

Cynthia wondered, 'So what do we do now?'

'Greyrivers is arranging a carriage for us to return to Totteringstate. I cannot see him for want of this crowd.'

'Aye, crowds are not pleasant.' Cynthia attempted to sound like a local, but her accent needed more work.

'No, no they are not,' I agreed.

Soon enough, I spotted the good Captain waving at us above the crowd, calling out. We went closer and saw a smartly coloured coach with plush insides, and a chamber pot. Mr Amos, after packing away our kit, sat atop with the driver and the three of us gathered ourselves inside. Our home was not far from here, however, with coach travel, it felt like an eternity.

Greyrivers mused, "Tis so good for you to be returning home, Willec?'

'I find it so.'

'I cannot wait to meet your family, my love,' Cynthia sounded impatient.

I firmly believed my family would get on with her, as they should do, compared to the short time I had dealing with Cynthia's lot.

'Oh,' Greyrivers commented, 'I heard the grandfather was finally disposed of. I had word on the ship; it gets around, you know.'

'Yeah?' My mind perked up... *that confrontation at the State House.* I let out a sigh, not batting an eyelid. The family was spreading anti-British sentiment in their region. He deserved the consequence... *they all did, that cowardly bunch!*

'As you helped deliver the rebels into our hands, you might meet the King.' Greyrivers sounded hopeful.

'Me?' I mouthed.

'Well, you helped stay the rebellion and save our colonies.'

'We did,' Cynthia chimed in, expressing pride in her achievement... *our achievement.*

Yes, we did. I felt something in my red outer uniform coat. I dipped my hand in one of the pockets therein and realised I still possessed the instrument of their destruction. *Their snooty declaration.* It was still there. I had forgotten about it on the ship's voyage and had a better read of it during the rest of our time in the carriage. Cynthia and the Captain had an amicable chat. I smiled as I read the content of the rebel document and found it to be frivolous and provocative.

Greyrivers turned to me, 'Willec, you look possessed. What have you got there?'

I was unsure if I should reveal it, *but hey, why not?*

He was my brother-in-law and was just as much a part of the campaign as I was. I gave it to him, smiling.

'What? Is this funny to you?' The Captain was not privy yet to the hilarity the rebels thought they conveyed in writing.

'Have a read. It is even funnier when you see the bit they wrote about the slave trade.'

A short silence was kept as Greyrivers scanned the document. He smiled and handed it back to me, 'I think the King will need to read this, too. He'll get a kick out of it.'

'Yea, he will,' I concurred, 'This is the proof of the rebel's treason against our rule. Cynthia, here, had done us a marvel. You should have seen the look of the congressmen's faces as she snatched the paper away from them to give to us. Most of them looked like they could use a chamber pot by that point.'

We laughed maniacally, as if we were telling a funny joke. Well, we were... *or so we thought.* I was very proud of Cynthia for sticking it to those *so-called* great men. Actually, Dr Franklin *was* truly great, as his intellect and acumen of invention showed in the past. *Yet, he decided to cast his lot with this... it was appalling.* Those fellows will spend time banging their silly gavels in the Tower or possibly hanging out by their seams.

I folded up the document to return it to its rightful place within my coat. It should be safe there and I will have to keep it, if I am to show it to the King.

As Totteringstate was getting closer, I noted the rugged roads were becoming quite passable and cleared through by various grounds men to allow carriages by on their many journeys (*we so liked to travel!*).

My other two companions had nodded off for a bit, whilst I remained restless and did not bother. The gentle suspension of the carriage was a nice way to lull oneself.

I must say that it took so long on these trips, and I found them a right nuisance. *I wished there was a faster way to go...*

Approximately a half hour later, according to my pocket watch, we reached the great Hall. Cynthia and Greyrivers stirred in their places to the sound of livestock noises from the distance of Dumfushire, the neighbouring county to ours. Bird noises were most welcome to my ears as I began to get myself in order.

'Ready for the off, my little Cynthia?' *I so loved to tease the girl.*

'I think so. You know, this area of yours reminds me of Scatsville,' she said.

'Rural idylls are similar in most places. What makes them differ is those who live in them and you will be happy to know that **they** do not live here.'

Cynthia let go a really heavy sigh. She felt the calm and coolness that Woolanshire had to offer.

The carriage had come to a stop by the front door. I saw my dear twin, Lottie, with his new wife, Daffnette, sitting on the front porch bench talking... *possibly waiting for us.*

I left the coach, whilst our stuff was being gathered up by Mr Amos, and went up to them.

'Long time, eh?'

Lottie looked up, 'Willec! You've returned in one piece. Thank God. I prayed very hard for you... gosh, it's so good to see you.'

My twin can be very melodramatic.

We hugged on another and Daff approached me.

'You're back, then. How did it go?'

'The best man wins, but no mean feat.'

I gave Daff a hug when Cynthia and Greyrivers came up. I took Cynthia by the hand to introduce her.

Greyrivers came up to me first, (before I had chance to introduce Cynthia) and told me he needed to go back to Sydmouth to his family. I bade him farewell and shook his hand.

"Til we meet again, I will miss you, Willec. It had been a good voyage with you,' the Captain said to me.

'Will miss you too... and thank you.'

He walked off to the carriage and drove it back to the Harbour. Mr Amos took our stuff into the house.

I resumed my intention with Cynthia and brought her to Lottie and Daff.

'Who's that?' I sensed a slight jealous ring to Daff's voice.

I whispered in her ear, 'Not now Daff, not in front of Lottie. You've got him now.'

I then introduced the new one to our circle, 'This is Cynthia, my wife. Cynthia, this is Lottie, my twin brother and his wife Daffnette.'

'Hello, Cynthia. Welcome to our home,' Lottie said, most kindly.

'Pleased to meet you both,' she extended her hand out, which both shook respectively. I felt a slight apprehension from Daff.

'Willec, can we talk?'

I turned to Daff, 'Yes. Let's go to the bench yonder.' We walked to the far end of the garden for privacy, as Cynthia and Lottie got to know each other... *well, we were now family, after all.*

'What is your matter, Daff? You seem unsettled.'

'Willec. You know I wanted you from the beginning and to find you with someone else...,' she whinged.

'You should not worry about me, now that you've got Lottie. Greyrivers told me you'd decided to marry him.'

'I know. It was at your father's insistence, as we did not know when you would return, IF you returned.'

'War is a many splendour'd thing,' I quipped, 'I warned you not to wait up for me. I was very lucky. I only received a shoulder wound.'

'Can I see?' *Silly Daff, why would you want to?!*

I took off the red coat, unbuttoned the waistcoat, and loosened the shift, revealing the bandage which remained on me for a while. *I'd forgotten all about it, and it needed changing.* Daff had a different look on her face when she saw the wound.

'I am so sorry,' she said, downcast, 'So, you are planning to marry this Cynthia?'

'We had already married over there. I so loved her, and with my help, she broke the ties. Look, Daff, she has been through a lot. We plan to renew our vows properly and begin our lives afresh.'

'Am I invited?'

'Course you are. I insist; but I humbly confess to you, I do not love you. I really like you as a friend and hope we can remain so, especially as you are now part of our family, as is Cynthia. You will have many duties to help run the parish with Lottie and that should keep ye busy. Please do not fret over our past. It is what it is and we cannot change it.'

'You're right again, Willec. I also noticed you brought along a coloured fellow.'

'Yes, I did. He was a runaway slave. Now, he is one of us. Besides, Fantasie needs a companion, and,' I cleared my throat, 'you know...' I smiled. Daffnette squealed.

'I feel better already,' she admitted, admiring the matchmaking work I performed.

'Good. Now, you get along with Cynthia. She is a loving and important person. After all, she helped save our colonies.'

'Saved our colonies?' Daff laughed even louder, so loud that in the distance, I could see Lottie and Cynthia turning their heads towards us.

'Yea, it's a long story. Please, let us go back to the Hall.'

'Does she have any family?'

'Aye, she does... ME!' I said sternly, and walked off toward home.

'Willec, I did not mean...,' Daff was clutching at straws again... she really had issues, as I'd feared. *That is why I married Cynthia.*

She caught up with me as we joined my brother and Cynthia and went into the Hall.

'Willec, I'm sorry. It came out so poorly... I let go again, didn't I?'

'You did,' I said, still in stern-mode.

Daff turned to Cynthia in desperation, 'Friends?' She stuck out her hand.

Cynthia accepted, 'Thank you. I would really like that.' *So polite, yes!*

We proceeded to the salon where a tea service was set up for us by Fantasie and Mr Amos. I trusted he'd met her whilst we were chatting outside. He is entitled to do his own introduction. He may be a *slave* as such, but I would rather treat him properly, with dignity and not like shit the way his former owners treated him... *much like Cynthia and her family.* We had our refreshment, chattering away like old friends, then departing to our respective apartments.

Cynthia enjoyed her time here, in the meantime. Although she was like a clumsy wheel at Totterningstate, I had faith that she would smooth out.

Mother had approached me and we embraced.

'She's a nice girl, Willec.'

'I know. She's a right cracker.' I then took Mother aside and sparsely explained Cynthia's former circumstances and how she helped our Cause. Mother gasped, raising her hand to her mouth in awe.

'That poor girl,' she moaned… *imagine if she heard the rest of it!*

'Yes, so please do not press on about the colonies or family. It would be most appreciated. She is still aggrieved by the situation she had been put in and is proud of correcting the same by marrying me. Don't discuss any of it at all, unless it is between you and her, alone,' I begged.

She agreed to the discretion with all her care and attention.

Later on, Lottie and I met in the library, where I showed him Cynthia's paperwork of her time *over there*. He looked through it with great interest.

'So, what happened to her after her old baptism to the time of her renewal of Christian vows?'

I whispered in his ear, 'Her grandparents took custody of her when her mother died, and the father, who was a Catholic, was chased away. They raised her as Jewish.'

'Wow,' Lottie said, 'So she is...'

'No,' I coarsely interrupted, 'She is not, as evident here. She was pushed into it against her will; unasked, and assumed, just because her mother's family did it. The family actually were non-Jews posing as Jews and this began only a couple of generations previous to the grandparents. Cynthia was a child and thus coerced into living a lie. She did not *choose* to be Jewish, for narrow minds in a big world do not mix.'

'Was there proof of this so-called lie?'

'That is the problem, there was no proof, and with no proof, there is dubiousness. Most information we received was from people we interrogated in the area with regard to this. Some of them had come forward out of revenge, because Cynthia's family were causing problems. They were spreading anti-British sentiment and most of the locals remained with us. This was our mission; to get that girl out of there and deal with the rebel community to which that family belonged.'

Lottie acknowledged the information with a nod. Daff walked down the corridor toward the door and tried to listen in, gently leaning on the door to snatch bits of my discussion with Lottie. Mother at this point passed by her.

'Daff, could you please come with me? I need you to help with some embroidery I'm working on.'

Daff could not resist a good embroidery session, 'Sure, Hermanda.' She left the door and went to another room with Mother. Mother was good like that. She knew what Lottie and I were up to and *it was better for Daff to remain in ignorance to the same.*

Back inside, I arranged for Cynthia's confirmation, as the next step in her Christian instruction, as well our nuptial vow renewal. It will be a splendid affair and I could not wait to renew my desire for her.

Chapter XII

The months that followed our return were a hubbub of activity. Cynthia was carefully instructed by Lottie for her confirmation service, and, later, we both undertook the renewal of the vows we made in New York, so our loved ones and friends may see the commitment we made to one another (*and that we meant it, too!*). However, word got out about it and soon, Totteringstate Parish was brimming with many from far and wide to witness the event.

We took a holiday (for our honeymoon) to Sydmouth Harbour for good refreshment and stayed with my sister Emmadayle. Captain Greyrivers was on another mission for His Majesty's Pleasure (probably to help subdue the colonies, now that they were back under *our* control). Sydmouth was lovely on a cool day, with the River Syd calmly floating on by. There were ships moored in the Harbour awaiting passage; people and goods hurrying to and fro upon wooden planked boarding. There were shoppes filled with sea-themed souvenir trinkets, along with places to eat, drink and be amused.

Cynthia and I spent a fortnight here and we both loved it. She'd caught the sun on her face, despite the broad brimmed bonnet she wore. I was only too happy to be out of uniform and formality. I really let myself go to enjoy the time spent, as far as the age allowed.

Our relations were progressing romantically well and Cynthia began to show a small bump beneath a new floral gown I bought for her. *Ah, how she loved her floral designs!*

We carried on our promenade, when we caught a glimpse of outdoor theatrics featuring two lovers having a petty tiff. It looked all too interesting and already, the troupe's duo had gathered up a fine audience. We only heard this bit of dialogue by the time we'd arrived.

'Do not go to sea, my Captain, you must stay, anon, and marry me!' the lady begged.

The Captain responded, 'I cannot, for any reason, wish to stay, for my Country's at war and I must fight for same.'

'If fight you must, go forth, see sense, and come back to me,' she cried.

'If I choose not to go, I shall be in trouble, sore deep. Shall I arrange another meeting hence. Perchance, shall I declare my love for you, and then to face my expiration alone?'

'No, I shall not hav'it. You are mine... you are not al--,' she proceeded to fall from the stone rampart, hoping her Captain would catch her in safety.

He rushed up to her and screamed, 'Jaaaannneeee!'

He tried to break her fall, but her plump stature caused them both to collapse in a pile of confusion. The Captain's head hit the ground, resulting in a minor concussion (and it took awhile to get him 'round again). The crowd gasped and after a short while, he came to and adlibbed, 'So, how was it?'

'You make a fine cushion, James,' she said, and they kissed fervently.

The scene had ended. The crowd applauded and the two actors bowed to receive their thanks. All there had dispersed and Cynthia and I made our way to the local.

'That was funny,' she commented.

'A free play is most worthy to see,' I replied, donating a shilling to the dispensary box to help the actors along with their laughs.

'Why, thank ye, sir. 'Tis most kind,' the 'Captain' said.

I saluted back at him and we carried on. We had a quick pint between the two of us and made our way back to Emmadayle's.

* * * * * *

After our return to Totteringstate, I was informed of a letter in my in-folio in the study, formerly used by Father (and now used by myself). I had a good look at it. Square in shape, crisply neat handwriting, and addressed to:

Colonel William Alexander Woodes-Hastings
Totteringstate Hall
Totteringstate
Woolanshire

I reversed the paper and saw the seal had a faint coat of arms. I honestly could not imagine who it could be, as all my friends would have used a more militaristic style. I broke it and proceeded to read the message. Before I got into the text, I rechecked the seal and tried to recover it. *Damn, unable to do so.* I walked over to the window seat which let in more light to read by and found I was wanted by a most High Order.

To Colonel W A Woodes-Hastings
From His Majesty George III, King of Great Britain and Ireland
Sir:
Your attendance is requested at Court on the 17th October 1777 at 10'o clock in the Forenoon, St. James' Palace, for Decoration and Honour, Amongst your Peers, For your Actions in the Suppression of the Late Rebellion in the North American Dominions.
Windsor
September 6, 1777
9 past 9 AM

WOW! It was from the King... THE King. I was so honoured. I raced for my desk to acquire my quill and parchment and I scribbled a quick reply:

To His Majesty, George III, King of Great Britain and Ireland
From Colonel W A Woodes-Hastings
Your Majesty:
Could I Bring My Wife to Your Court? She Helped Us in Our Struggle.
Totteringstate
September 15, 1777

To which he replied some days later:

From His Majesty George III, King of Great Britain and Ireland
From Colonel W A Woodes-Hastings
Sir:
Yes, By All Means, Bring Her. I Insist. We All Want to Meet the Saucy Wench who Saved My Colonies and, What's More, She Saved Many of Our Lives by Not Letting the Rebellion Linger a Moment Past the Hour.
Windsor
September 25, 1777
12 past 8 AM

Well, that was it. Cynthia was to be introduced to *The King!* All her efforts paid off and her suffering was not in vain. I found her doing embroidery with Mother.

She looked up at me to ask, 'What news, Willec?'

'We have been requested at St. James' Palace on October 17 to attend the King's Court.'

She stared at me and freaked out, 'WHAT? I do not believe this. The King wants to meet *me?*'

Mother, in her no-nonsense, countrified manner, quipped, 'You'd best be going, then.' She gave a wry smile at us.

Her comment and smile sparked a couple of minutes silence and Cynthia and I squealed with laughter.

'That's it, then; we've made it,' she commented.

I replied, 'Yea, looks that way, doesn't it?'

The next few weeks will be our most busiest together, preparing for an Audience and Honour from the King.

* * * * * *

We had an arrival from Court to Totteringstate Hall to give Cynthia and I lessons on court etiquette, conversation skills (mostly for Cynthia, as she lacked adequacy in this bit), and, of course, ballroom dancing. It was a lively few weeks before we headed off and in the duration of time, it had been a very tottering state around here, indeed.

We left a week before our meeting, to allow for the rubbish roads and lanes we'd have to pass. Some of my friends in the regiment went ahead, as they, too, were called to court. Some of them like Cateliffe and Nay-Smith had provided escort guard for our carriage to ensure a safe passage. *No standing 'round here; we shall not deliver, thank you very much!*

It took several days for us to arrive in London and the King allowed us to share space with his horsemen at Windsor. Cynthia and I remained together and the rest of my fellow soldiers bunked it out with the rest within the grounds of the great Castle.

At St James' Palace, we met The King... His Majesty King George III. He was seated on a dais on the far side of the audience chamber. There was a tenseness in the air, as is expected when one meets Royalty, first time. The Queen sat beside him and both looked like a formal pair of bookends, without the books in between. The room was curtained in a lavish dark velvet, framing large sash windows which overlooked some formal gardens. It was fanciful, but in a plain way.

He took a shine to Cynthia and began an earnest conversation. My face begat a quizzical look.

The King glanced at me and asked, 'Colonel, is there something wrong? You look concerned.'

'No, Your Majesty,' I replied, 'I have something of great importance that you need to see, and in acquiring the same, we need to thank this girl you are currently engaged in conversation with.'

The King turned to Cynthia, 'I trust he means you.'

'Your trust is in the right place,' she said, coolly.

That's my girl, she's learning! Woo-hoo! Daff would never have pulled that off.

I gave the Rebel document to a pageboy who, upon receiving the same, took it up to His Majesty and gave it to him on a silver platter.

'Why thank you, Nivvie, you may go,' He said to the boy, turning to me, 'Do excuse me whilst I go a-fluff.'

George III began to read the document. The arguments contained therein were nonsense to Him, but as soon as he reached the clause relating to the slave trade, he let out a rapturous laugh upon reading the very same. A hushed pause broke out for Him to take it all in.

'They've got to be kidding,' He exclaimed. 'They curse me for allowing the slave trade to continue and as such, they have the nerve to perpetuate this on their own doorstep. Now, how hypocritical is that, what what?? WHAT!?'

The brutal hilarity came to a sudden end when it occurred to everyone in the room these colonists meant business; they listed all the 'crimes' against them by our government. It was the work of an extremist, a hothead, and a clever one, indeed. *Thus, we had to put a stop to it, for not all over there felt this way.*

'I must say, Colonel, their Opposition can be Most Eloquent,' The King commented, upon reflection after reading their *Declaration*.

'Agreed, Your Majesty,' I followed on, 'In fact, it can also be Most Dangerous. Imagine the old orders crumbling down upon rhetoric like this. My God, that would be the End of Our Way of Life!'

The King stated, 'Yea, if this got out, my boy, I would not be sitting pretty here, now would I?' He then looked at Cynthia, tenderly querying, 'My dear, how do you feel about all this, hey hey, what?'

'My liege, I feel that--,' she got cut short.

A more personal side was revealed to us when The King interrupted impatiently, 'No No NO! Please, I know we've just met, but please, call me George.'

An embarrassed silence was further felt. Those around The King were flabbergasted at the request. Cynthia kept her cool, 'What about your other names, William or Fredrick?'

'You call me George. There is already a William and a Fredrick, who are their Royal Highnesses, eh eh?' He smiled at her.

'Thank you,' she curtsied.

'You must have been my biggest fan in the colonies, knowing my other Christian names, what the what?'

'I have Endeavoured to be True to Your Cause and I have Brokered the Document, which You Hold before You, into Your Safe Hands. As well as you know, it would be the Most Dangerous Instrument of All Time...an Instrument of Mass Destruction for Our Order.'

The King smiled, 'My good girl, we will need to talk further.' He then turned to me, 'Colonel, I mean, what do they like to call you?'

'Willec, Sir!' I stood firm, saluting.

'Willec, then... now look me in the eye and tell me where you received such a Beautiful and Intelligent Specimen from. I want to know all about her. I want her to be ---,' now it was the King's turn to get interrupted.

'George!' Queen Charlotte exclaimed, coming over to him, knowing His Majesty went off now and again in excitement. 'Know your place!'

The King looked at His Wife, 'Yes, Dear,' he succumbed. *She was a tough touch*, he thought, *but I guess that is why I had to marry her...*

Cynthia tried her best to continue, but waited for His Majesty, as she was taught earlier at Totteringstate.

'Ah, yes, so sorry about that my girl, do go on,' He said, still smiling. *Do go on...*

She stood militarily at attention, 'The colonial hotheads would storm and siege, they'll kill the king, and commence violence in the streets, sir.' She saluted and did another curtsey.

The King ranted, covering past events, 'Well, That cannot happen. What What!! We are not a revolutionary country, by far, no no no. We are known for Quiet Revolutions... yes yes yes... William and Mary, 1688 and all that what business. Our two man band... what what what?! It was sad with them. Mary got the pox and William got off his horse the hard way. Then there was Anne, the childless wonder... too bad her only surviving son passed. No, we must keep ourselves in Order, or there will be more to pay than molehills and deadly childbirths.'

Cynthia put her hand to her stomach, obvious to her condition.

'Are you pregnant, my dear? What what what would it be, a boy or a girl?! Eh, eh??'

Most of the company in the room so far had showed signs of boredom toward The King's endless chatter with the former colonist. They resented the sudden interest in her, even the passing familiarities. *No, no, that would not do...* but, they gave The King His Due. After all, His Colonies were still His, as a result of *her* actions, which were comparable to actions of fighting soldiers... and some off course conversations within the room turned to the 'enthusiasm' she'd displayed in the Name of the Cause.

Cynthia answered, 'I do not know what sex the child will be. I will just be thankful if it survives.'

The King concurred with her sentiment, 'Yes, a surviving child is worth more than meets the eye, what-ho!'

The room settled down as the ceremonies got underway. I was duly knighted for my Actions in the Late Rebellion and entitled as Sir William Alexander Woodes-Hastings, Lord of Totteringstate. Cynthia was hence known as Lady Woodes-Hastings, and interestingly enough, engaged in employment as The King's Minder. I, too, was engaged by His Majesty to be in the Household Calvary. I had a feeling we would be away from Totteringstate for good chunks on end... *and that will make it easier to forget about Daffnette and for her to get on with her life with Lottie.*

My friend, Major-General Wolfe-Harris was now known as Lord Sydmouth, and my friends Buckingham, Nay-Smith and Cateliffe all were allowed to have 'Sir' put in front of their names. There were other awards, knighthoods and formal acknowledgements given to other members present at the Court. I was just pleased with a title placed upon my very existence!

Chapter XIII

It had been over a year since our initial meeting with the King and our commencing appointments to serve Him. I did my time with the Horse Guards, and, as well as myself, Tarleton, Simcoe and Rawdon had joined me from their respective regiments as *they were the best of the lot.* After their rough stint in the Colonies, he rewarded them by transferring them from possible distant posts to serve Him personally. My long-time friends, Cateliffe, Nay-Smith and Buckingham had been reassigned elsewhere.

Cynthia spent much time with His Majesty during her gestation period; He knowing all too well what it is like to have a child. They conversed on many subjects, but what pressed Cynthia was concern for her unborn child. The King eased her discomfort and the company, on both sides, was proved most helpful.

On one occasion, she and the King had gone on walkabout through the grounds of Windsor Castle. It was cloudy and chilly, yet tolerable for a walk-around.

'I've got many other palaces, you know,' He said.

'Yeah?' Cynthia thought this sounded like a Right Royal pick-up line. *He must have dozens of them.*

'Buckingham House, Kew, Richmond, this place,' he gestured toward Windsor, 'for starters.'

'I bet they'd charge some mean admission rates.'

George III laughed, 'My dear Cynthia, they are not open to the public.'

'Too bad, but at least you've room for your growing family.'

'Yes, that I do... however,' He whispered, 'I can grant you fair passage.'

'Even I have never seen underpants blowing in the wind.'

'Neither have I and I believe there is a Fly on the Broadcast. We must clear it up, what what?!'

They both laughed as Queen Charlotte got off a nearby bench and came up to them, unaware of their past exchange and assuming the worst.

'You big shot American... here, cavorting with His Majesty,' she said in distain.

'I am NOT American,' Cynthia protested, 'And thanks to me, America does not exist! *You* still own it.'

'You may be The King's Minder, at His Majesty's Pleasure, but you go too far. You must know your place, young lady!'

The King snapped, 'She certainly does know her place, My Queen, and so do I. You would not be sitting on your bench over there, if it were not for her. There are powder kegs of hotheads just waiting to cut the throats of their respective kingdoms. There could be a revolution, what what?? And would you like that, eh???' His already large blue eyes bulged squarely toward her like miniature planets.

The Queen scoffed, 'Your Majesty is insane!'

'Am I? I am only insane due to the Knowledge of Affairs and State and its Burdens and Responsibilities. This girl, here, has done nothing to you nor has hurt you. In fact, she literally *saved* us!'

He paused to catch his breath, then continued, 'She is keeping me in check, I am keeping my government in check and you are due for another baby. So, if I were you, Ma'am, I would not take the Order for granted. We are finally a Stable Nation. I will not yield to your demands. The Balance of our Kingdom has been restored and she saved many lives of our Forces.'

'Only for those said Forces to go and die elsewhere in Your Service.'

'Yea, but at least Cynthia restored My Service! She has kept me balanced for some time and I will not let her go.'

'Who's to stop me? I know of her dealings over there,' The Queen challenged.

'What dealings? If you are on about that Indian Raid, I knew about that earlier. I get word, you know, what what. You do not even know what really happened. There was sedition in the area, which led to the capture of the Rebel document,' The King answered back.

'Either way, your 'girl' must know her place.' To Cynthia, she spat, 'Peasant!'

'I'm Lady Woodes-Hastings, now,' Cynthia defended.

'How dare you call my 'girl' a peasant. I would not allow peasants in my presence, thank you very much. You German woman, you are too forceful. I am The King, not you! What what!'

The Queen cooled down a bit, but stood her ground, 'I still say you ARE insane.'

'Tell it to the judge, Ma'am. I say you are a callous, cruel woman.

'As we will be together for a while and you two being pregnant, I say to make up your differences right here, right now. Imagine a King who controls an Empire cannot control the female bits of his household, what now?' He scoffed.

Queen Charlotte and Cynthia went up to each other to shake hands, begrudgingly.

'Sorry I caused you a menace,' The Queen said.

'I have nothing against you, Ma'am. I just wish my time over there was not brought up. What happened to me was not my doing. That family, who did what they did to me, were spreading unrest in the local area, and rebelling against Your Royal Persons. I stood up for you in the midst of that stupid Congress, as they call it,' Cynthia explained.

The Queen's attitude took a radically different turn, 'I heard about what you did in front of that *Congress* and I commended you on the same.' She put her arm around Cynthia, 'Look, I was just testing you. I needed to know that you really are as tough as everyone described you as. We cannot just let *anyone* into our fold, you know.'

Cynthia reflected, 'I appreciate your discourse in your knowledge of me, albeit second hand. I believe being among your soldiers and marrying one helped close the coffin on fear and haste.'

'I can see you take care of The King well and He seems to be taken by you. You do His Mind a service and He can rest at night knowing His Own Confidences and Strength.'

'Ma'am, if it weren't for me, you might not have a King.'

They reconciled with a hug and The Queen said, 'Welcome to Our Family. I know you will have one of your own soon, but you will always have a place with us.'

'As if Your Family isn't packed enough as it is,' Cynthia jested.

'Ah, well, the more, the merrier and more secure Our Reign, no?'

'Makes sense, I guess.'

Cynthia blushed with satisfaction, knowing *her* place. It was beside The King. It was also beside *me*.

* * * * * *

Cynthia's time was nigh and I felt we needed to return to Totteringstate to have our child. The King saw our situation as personal and gave us due indefinite leave to deal with the growing family. His wife, The Queen, was also near time and He would be occupied with all that, and, along with matters of State, He stated to us that He will be just fine on His own, *for the time being*. He insisted we keep in touch in the meantime and keep Him informed of our progress and welfare. It would be likely I would be called back to the equerry, and when Cynthia and the baby are stable, she could likely return to her post by His side.

Thankfully, Totteringstate was not too far from London but it still took some time for our return. I wrote to my immediate friends to inform them and that they were invited over, should they wish to visit. The overall response was that they could get away for a bit, as we all knew one another, it was good they were able to attain their leave.

Cynthia was as comfortable as she could be, and when the time came, Fantasie assisted her in the birth. She was no midwife, but she knew a thing or two about childbirth, having witnessed it from whence she came.

Cateliffe, Nay-Smith and Buckingham also lent a hand, if not moral support, and when the child was delivered, it was a healthy 7.5 pound baby girl. We named her Cynthia Rose; Cynthia, for the mother and Rose, because she looked very red and a very English Rose she was, indeed (*at least by my lineage*). The child cried upon exiting its former home, being cast out into the world, but, at least, into the arms of most loving parents.

I was so elated at the moment, and by Cynthia's side, I was able to see the child immediately and hold her in my arms. What a lovely pink glow she emitted! I was most pleased to have a girl. There will be time for boys... eventually.

The christening of our Cynthia Rose Woodes-Hastings took place at Totteringstate Parish and Lottie did the ceremony. He and Daffnette also served as godparents to the little mite. Mother was happy for me and gave me a loving kiss. My friends congratulated me and Cynthia held the baby in her arms with pride. *Pride... and the freedom to give to Cynthia Rose to be what she chooses to be, not to be told what to be.* She let me hold little Rose and, wow, to have the baby in my arms was absolutely euphoric. It was more than a soldier could emotionally bear and this gave me a good reason to stick to my calling. *I now had something to really fight for.*

It was a most blessed moment for our family as our little Rose blossomed well over the weeks following the birth. She was well-cared for, bottles at the ready, plenty of blankets, pillows and toys. We wheeled her round the Hall to show her little aspects of our dynasty and to what she was entitled.

Cynthia Rose had absorbed the information and looked around with interest. We did not inform her about her mother's history, as that was off-limits for the time being. I needed to entrench her as a Woodes-Hastings and when she attained a reasonable age, the rest of the history will be revealed to her, *in small amounts*.

We had regular visitors to Totteringstate over the time as well. Good wishers from the nearby villages and those who came all the way from Dumfushire to give us the best regards. Everyone who got to see the child and were amazed on how beautiful she was. Cynthia, the mother, was going along with everything and adjusting to motherhood naturally. Although the birth took much out of her (aside from just the baby and accompanying bits), she became rather passive in the year since her relocation. The earlier spunk and enthusiasm she had shown in an earlier day had ebbed away steadily, as she integrated well into our society and *better way of life*. There were times she had to be forgiven of the old ways when they had returned, but they, like a quickening houseguest, took leave. She returned to a calmer state, ready to continue in the saddle of motherhood.

It had been some weeks to let the hubbub die down and I took some time to write to The King.

I informed him of our newest family member, Cynthia Rose, weighing 7.5 pounds and that mother and child are prospering.

A month or so later, I received His news: *We've got a daughter too, Sophie Matilda, what what! All is well. GR*

My relations with Cynthia increased again and shortly after, she was slightly inconvenienced. She took it in stride and I was itching to return to soldiering, if not the equerry. I wrote to The King again to inform him of my interest, as well as Cynthia's being pregnant again and he told me to remain at Totteringstate and take care of the wife.

He did recommend further training exercises at the local HQ, (where I was when I trained for our mission to New York), to keep occupied and, later, to join the militia, where I served for the next few years.

In the meantime, our family expanded again (during my times on leave), as child after child was born during this period. I finally had a boy, Cedric Brian, another little girl we called Mary Emma, followed by another boy, Leslie Thomas. They all were thriving nicely, as did Cynthia Rose, under the continuing auspices of Mother and Cynthia. Even Daff and Fantasie helped out when they could.

After our considerable absence, Cynthia and I returned to our Posts in The King's Service. The King's family, too, had grown also, so He was obviously occupied. I returned to the stables where I found my old friend Tarleton and fellow comrades Simcoe and Rawdon carrying out their equerrian duties. Tarleton and I took a breather and went outside the stables.

'I heard about your family. Some brood you've got there,' he said, 'It must have taken much time to look after that lot.'

'Aye,' I agreed, 'The King was most generous, yet, it was also out of His Need too.'

'Oh?'

'He has a family as well to look after.'

'Oh, yes, yes, I know that. His Majesty would not be very generous to just anybody, you know. You are most fortunate.'

'I say I am,' I laughed, 'Our Cynthia Rose is already like her mother; the others are far more quieter.'

'Uh-oh,' Tarleton laughed and proposed, 'You'll have another enthusiastic soul on your hands. Perhaps if we can train her...'

I thought about it, but a female Dragoon, even with enthusiasm, would not make it. From our standpoint, *women just did not fight!*

I kidded around with him anyway, 'Does your company allow little big mouthed girls?'

'Yea, if they can fight as hard as they speak.'

'Nah, allow her Spirit to grow... we can make use of it another way. Don't want her mixed up in anything.'

'If she is how you describe her, she will find her own Causes to get mixed up in.'

'As long as the Causes are Ours,' I chuckled, with attentive certainty.

'Would she be keen to serve The King?' Tarleton seemed hopeful.

'Probably, and with a mouth like hers, she can also serve Parliament, for all I care! I think His Majesty would be very taken with her character.'

'And what a character she is,' Tarleton continued his mirth, 'Why don't you get them down here sometime, then?'

'I will have to speak to His Majesty about that,' I sighed. *If Cynthia Rose was becoming like her mother and she and The King were to meet...*

I excused myself and took a walk in the Gardens. I saw The King and Cynthia, my wife, in the distance.

I regarded my family back home... our children were being looked after by Fantasie, Mother and Daffnette. Daffnette enjoyed helping and though she and Lottie had yet to breed their own, it was just as pleasurable to look after our juveniles.

* * * * *

It was the early 1780s. The Colonies we fought to keep, remained in our possession and lost their errant ways. The initial troublemakers were weeded from society and those we've captured were nearly forgotten about... until I had a wicked idea with regard to them. I discussed this with my dearest Cynthia, who thought well of it.

'So what do you plan, my lord?'

'Remember your little speech in front of the Congress when you referred to 'His Majesty's Display'?'

'Yes, I do,' she recalled, 'I was referring to having them in stocks or just showing them off like an animal display... to see the so-called Great Minds reduced to the Humiliated States of America.'

'Alright, but I was thinking of writing about our exploits in America as a play and calling it *In Defence of Our Colonies*.'

'Splendid... wait, you are a soldier, you have no artistic license!'

'Ah, that is where you are wrong, my dear.' I then explained to her I expressed an early interest in the arts, but that was quashed when the Seven Years' War broke out and I was called to serve. I so loved the little secrets I kept hidden and they became a surprise for Cynthia, as I revealed more of myself to her in due course.

On my off times from soldiering, I got to writing and I had Nay-Smith, Cateliffe, and even Tarleton in on it. We decided to give some of the roles to the prisoners but some of them protested. They relented, of course, for it was either that or public execution (as they did commit *treason* against us). They played themselves, as they were when we found them in their State House. We played our roles, as we experienced, in the reality of being *over there*.

Nay-Smith offered to play Crazypaws in his absence. Other roles went to very confident drama students who went to play extras and even some members of Cynthia's previous family. I did have to tread lightly as to how much information I was to give, in respect to the play and, where confidentiality was still present, I had to tailor it to make it more palatable to our audiences. *I made it so the Indian Raid was done due to seditious activity, and not due to religion.* In reality, *that* was true anyway, as we had to get Cynthia removed from the activities of her family, religious or seditious. It did not matter. *We knew what it was about and were not going to give **that** game away.*

We finally completed the play and gave it a run-through in front of The Royal Family (for they provided a big enough, yet intimate, audience!). It was a good way to test it live to see if it would win the hearts and minds of our fellow subjects. It was not a long endurance, just about an hour's worth of oddball memories of adventure and the like. We tried to include everything (save Cynthia's *private* business), and I think we did a good job of it. His Majesty was most impressed, as was His Queen and the Family. We held good favour with them.

After the performance, The Queen came over to Cynthia, with a bit more clarity, and said, 'So that's what you were up to over there. It must have been very hard for you.'

Cynthia curtsied before The Queen, 'Ma'am it was much harder than one thinks. This was the simplified version of a very complicated story.'

'Right. Well, good luck to you. Be well,' The Queen wished.

'Thank you, Your Majesty. I am most pleased you enjoyed our play.'

The King chimed in, most ardently, 'Yes, Yes, Yes! Bravo to you, Cynthia. Is that what your Speech was to the Congress?'

'As much as I could recall and Willec getting it down on paper,' she confessed.

'Boy, I would have loved to be there for THAT performance. *Young Lady Tells Congress Off!* God, I can see the broadsheets, what what?!'

Cynthia blushed fervently and said, 'I remember thinking about You as I did my little ditty in front of Congress. I said, 'If The King were here...,' and all that.'

'Yes, but... did you mean anything by that grenade bit? That is not like me, eh eh?' The King looked concerned.

'I think if you were put in the situation as I was, my Liege, I firmly believe You would wish a fully loaded arsenal aimed at the building itself.'

'Well, well, well, we'll not have that. Well, I wouldn't anyway. Do not you worry, your passion was not untoward,' George whispered, 'Actually, secretly, I wouldn't have minded a bit of that myself.'

'Oh, so the sentiments expressed were not unfavourable?'

'Not in the slightest... but I would have given them a *different* piece of One's Mind, what what!'

I finally went up to see Cynthia in His Majesty's Presence, as I was formerly occupied by other Royal well wishers, from the very young to the eldest Prince.

The King addressed me, 'That took much effort and love for me on your part. If there were more of you, I bet you would win wars against all the nay-sayers.'

Now I blushed and took it all in, 'If there was more of my wife around, the world could be put right in a day.'

'Well, what what what... you wish to beat God, do you?'

I was confuddled, 'Pardon?' It did take time to get used to The King's Speech.

'God made the Earth in seven days, so it says, and I wholeheartedly believe it. It takes many years or hours for things to go wrong. Your confidence in Cynthia must be quite strong for you to believe she can solve Worldly Issues in a Day.'

I squirmed inside, thinking I made a major faux pas, 'I do believe in Cynthia's capabilities and strengths. She has much to contribute.'

The King laughed and, thinking aloud, stated, 'We will have a Celebratory Dinner. You lot are invited. Come along with me.' He walked on, joining one of his younger children, the fair Amelia.

I stood there, looking a bit lowly in my stature, compared that with The King. It was kind of him to invite us to dinner. We kept the Appointment and whiled away a Gracious Evening.

* * * * * *

The play was performed at the Iseeum Theatre to rave reviews, especially since we added audience participation. We did not do this for the Royal run-through, but I thought it would be nice to be able to cause serious ridicule to our prisoners. After Cynthia's Most Glorious Speech, we had the audience pelt the prisoners with foodstuffs of every kind. Tomatoes and other squishy articles of the like proved best.

Yet, elsewhere, many speeches were being said, as the winds were changing and more hotheads emerged from the fold of society. One in particular was to become the Great Menace of Europe.

Chapter XIV

Across the way, in France, a young fellow was budding well in the military. Short in stature, yet big on ego, he stood above his comrades. He was unhappy at the State of Affairs with the rich getting richer and the poor continually being trampled upon in perpetuity. He looked around the streets. All was quiet on the Grande Rue de Soleil and the Bastille doors remained calm, too.

Napoleon Bonaparte was not someone to be trifled with. He was an angry cuss and hated the society he grew up in. The Royals and their flock remained at their illustrious posts of state, whilst bread shortages, along with further starvation, shadowed the populace like a dark cloud with a storm about to break. The only storm that did break, however, was Napoleon's Fury.

He had followers in his unit, and he ranted off wherever and whenever he cared to be heard by others. *Of course, who would listen to him?* There were a handful that heard his grievances and thought something should be done. The French King and Queen, for starters, should ease the taxation on the poor, so they could afford the merest amount, just to survive. *The King and Queen should do more for their people,* it was widely thought. Unfortunately, to many a person's knowledge, King Louis XVI was a dullard who liked to play with the locks around the palace and the Austrian, Queen Marie Antoinette, famously packed in as much retail therapy as the public purse would allow. The problem is... it *was* from the public purse... *as if she did not have any money of her own*, people would argue.

This is where Napoleon thought heavily about changing the Old Order. *The Ancien Regime needed to go*, he reckoned. He read books from Voltaire, Rousseau, texts from the Roman philosophers, military soldiers and some others. He was aware that the North American Colonies attempted to split from their Mother Country *and had failed.* Thus, Napoleon wanted to be the First Man to Change the Entire System... and throw away the Rule Book! A complete change, afresh with new ideas.

Maybe he could create a Republic where everyone would work together for the common good. It would include rich and poor alike. He would try to balance things so *everyone* could benefit. There would be no monarchy, so the Royals would need to go, but not necessarily to their deaths. *Perhaps exile?* It would take much thought on this. Napoleon had all the time in the world to create a world *he* wanted to live in... (*whether anyone else did, remained to be seen*).

* * * * *

Back in King George's Court, Cynthia was continuing her appointment with the King and giving him the all-important support and stability which allowed him to be a Great Monarch. However, there was much whispering at Court with regard to the King's Faculties. It did not seem much, but some conversations, overheard by others, had caused some sensation.

One of such conversations took place on an outdoor walk, which went like this:

'So, is there truth in the Light, Cynthia?'

She pondered the question, 'Depends on how bright or dim the Light is, I guess, Your Majesty.'

'Your Majesty no longer applies to you, dear, remember?'

'Oh, I know. I am not a Majesty.'

The King smiled, 'Very funny. You know what I mean!'

'I do, but it is sublime to be in Your Presence. I keep forgetting.'

'You are too humble,' He said.

'Comes from being put down all the time. I was concerned The Queen was going along the same lines as those who raised me.'

'Well, despite their faults and treasons, I think they did a good job. And you can take that all the way and back, what what!'

Cynthia blushed heavily. She never thought anyone would compliment her family's attempts in childrearing. She had to admit, *it did get her somewhere in life, even if it was away from them and into the presence of The King.*

'Stop blushing, girl! You might be mistaken for someone else, hey hey,' The King noted.

'I apologise and I cannot help it. I am not used to compliments, especially from someone like Yourself.'

'Well, get used to it, for you are a Fine Contributor to Our Society. What what!'

A pause commenced. The birds flew in the air, trees fluttered in the grand breezes that wrapped the afternoon in perfection.

The King went on, 'I heard your Willec saved a runaway slave. What did you think of slavery when you lived there?'

'Slavery was not an issue where I lived. I have seen many in shackles coming off the ships to new masters and lives. Willec was doing the fellow a favour cos he wanted to match him up with his girl at Totteringstate.'

'Willec's got a slave girl?'

'Yes, her name is Fantasie. He wanted her to have a companion and maybe breed for more people to help us out in the home and out in the Dumfushire pig farms.'

'Wow. So it was a mercy mission, in a way.'

'Merciful for whom? The poor fellow looked desperate. The first officer had allowed him aboard ship. Willec bought him off the officer. He's ours now and apparently doing well. We treat him with dignity and give him space with Fantasie, for, *you know*...'

'Yea, I know, what what! Wink Wink!' The King never showed such gaiety. Some people nearby looked at them with worry. They needn't have, though, as it was not untoward to show happiness to a subject. *Maybe there was a lack of understanding.* It was Cynthia's job to Ensure Understanding and to keep The King in Balance. Sometimes, it was agreeable to let go on occasion... such was the valve which let off compounding anxieties.

Cynthia smiled, seeing the real man emerge, but kept to subject, 'What do you think of the emerging Abolitionist Movement?'

He turned around, 'What do I think? I think they have good consciences and the good of the people in mind, but there will be many who will protest.'

'Why?'

"Tis an earned living, eh? People make profit off this.'

'But is it right?'

'Depends how much profit one makes, what what???!!'

'Maybe one day, they'll all be released into society and intermingle as they should, but it would be a mismatched culture clash, if there ever was one. It would take some getting used to.'

'Would you free yours?'

'I am sure Willec would make careful provision for them. He may keep them on as employees rather than slaves. It is all they know. They'd live on the premises and work alongside us.'

'Your Willec's got a goodly mind. You are a lucky wench to have picked him off like that. I heard he was promised to another.'

Cynthia was vexed when she thought about the *other* woman who her husband was *supposed* to marry. 'That is true, but his twin brother got her instead. I heard Willec did not even love the girl.'

'He was concerned for his career and did not want to break her heart.'

'Always the soldier first.'

The King suddenly began to sing, 'Primavosa, Saratoga, Modern Yoga, Everything Went!'

'Begging your pardon, I had no idea you could sing,' Cynthia exclaimed.

'I like to keep my talents hidden. Confusion of the many brings pleasure to the one. Ha-ha, what-ho!'

They laughed as more onlookers wanted to inform the Family of The King's Odd Behaviour. One of the Household dismissed the matter and dispersed the small crowd. Cynthia paid no mind to it as she was just as silly and understood where He was coming from.

He was just Releasing Himself to the Open Air. *No matter; no problem; no one gets hurt.*

* * * * *

Another incident occurred some time later.

'Your Majesty,' Cynthia called.

'Call me George, please, dear girl. We are friends now.'

'Your Majesty?'

'Call me George, or else...'

'Your Majesty,' she tried again.

'CALL ME GEORGE, WHAT WHAT!'

'Ah, that's what I was waiting for.'

'Why, are they on?'

The Queen walked past the Room where The King and Cynthia discoursed. She looked on, in despair, tearing out her hair... until she realised it was a wig.

* * * * *

The Royal Family, later on, were in the Drawing Room in their Palace.

'Papa is taking funny again,' little Octavius spoke out.

The Queen commented, 'I bet it's the Influence of Colonial Ways... always Under the Influence. I guess it takes one to know one.'

The Eldest Prince defended, 'It is not of any particular Influence at all. It is Papa, just Influencing himself. Cynthia supports Him during the Ranting, as it is let go of, and Papa can be Fresh of Mind, once more.'

'Well, whatever it is, this Behaviour is getting annoying, methinks,' She said.

Another Prince, Fredrick, piped up, 'It is The King's Prize, Mother. Cynthia won the Colonies back for us. It is Her Privilege to be with Papa. She can sort Him out.'

The Queen smirked, 'I think she is the only one who can deal with His Crazy Rants. I know I cannot stand His talking.'

'Well, Someone's got to Listen to Him and it is Her Job to do so,' another one of the Children spoke.

'Understanding someone goes a long way,' The Eldest Prince suggested, 'Maybe someday, she can sort me out.'

Fredrick teased, 'You definitely need sorting out,' and threw a close object toward His Royal Highness which hit the mark.

'FREDRICK!' The Queen spoke crossly, defending Cynthia's appointment, 'I wonder if it is YOU who needs sorting out. This ex-Colonial is doing Us a Good Service. Do not mock her.'

'We weren't, Mother,' The Elder Prince, 'We're just fooling about.'

'You can Fool About somewhere else,' The Queen snapped.

'But what about these Nonsensical Outbursts?'

'Never mind, they will blow over. We will let Cynthia do her job. She must endure this. Otherwise, we will have to get the mad doctor in and what is worse, he may resort to more punishing methods. I will not have My Husband go through that hell,' The Queen then recalled, 'With cupping, bleeding, and other Torturous Methods.'

'I hope you are right, Mother, or we will have a Bigger Problem than what we can cope with,' Prince William contributed, 'At least our side is Stable and the Colonies are in our possession still.'

* * * * * *

Napoleon always wanted to take the house down. The Royal House... at Versailles. He did not care about whether they were Bourbons or the Hapsburg Austrians. He envied them, but, unlike the poor, he never starved. Napoleon had the chance to study and he admired military heroes of the past, like Julius Caesar and Alexander the Great. He decided to be like his heroes and began his military career in an artillery regiment. He also became a Republican, devoted to the cause of Liberty. Napoleon thought to spread this message through military means. He disliked the Royals' lavish ways, whilst people starved in the streets. Napoleon was very mad about it, and this raving passion centred his focus. However, unlike the madman, he knew what he was doing.

On a sunny Saturday morning in 1789, during which everyone over a certain wage bracket was allowed to sleep in, he rose early for his attack upon the Grand Palace of Versailles. With a few friends and a few multitudes of followers, he stopped off at the Bastille to get more munitions, as well as asking if anyone would join him in the Cause of Freedom and Liberty.

Most of the 'Bastillions' had decided to cast their lot with Napoleon. After all, they had nothing to lose and, if the dear fellow won, they could leave their prison forever. They sided with him because he knew what he was doing. They felt freed from the shackled obligations and served their new Master.

Other troops followed the throng to make their way to Versailles. Versailles, the Grand Palace of many Louis. Napoleon wanted to be part of this grandeur, but anyone Less-Than-Royal, including himself, had no right to it. This did not remove the ambition from his determined brow to *become*. This is what he was after and, in time, he became his own Legend.

Despite the Palace being a Royal Home, it also served as a Royal Fortress, not unlike the predated castles of old. Yet, this 'Castle' yielded a secret and deadly weapon, so elusive, it needed the weather to activate its Weapon...

Back in the previous century, Louis XIV was known as 'The Sun King'. The Sun, being bright all round, was a reflection upon Louis as a shining object that one could not look upon for long. Not one for staring contests... he was a Real Legend and the longest serving Monarch to date. He relished in this dream of building something Regal, extending the old hunting lodge of his father, Louis XIII. He wanted to emulate the Sun, and be just as powerful. He had architects create this Gilded Palace with many windows, gold colours ingrained within the finery of detail, and with the forecourt depicting a light beige, sandy look. The entrance shone with golden gates, and a sun disk atop, showing a neutral face which needed no expression. The floors themselves looked as if they were paved in gold.

Louis XIV was very proud of his creation, and he loved living there, as well as holding Court. The best aspect of this Solar Fixation was that it prevented Versailles from Enemy Attack.

Every edificial pore of this Complex oozed with sunlight, which dazzled the eye, unaware. Louis, his immediate family, and descendants had all gloried in such a Palace. The current King Louis XVI had enjoyed the shade of its protection, knowing he and his own family would be safe within these sumptuous walls.

Not everyone knew this Secret. The poorer classes were oblivious, and those of Napoleon's well-to-do rank might have known, but dismissed it as Superstitious Nonsense. *Who would guess that Versailles was more than just a pretty face beside a forest moat?*

Napoleon, with his followers and troops, worked their way through the French Countryside. Some soldiers whinged about the endless heat. Others gathered their momentum and drudged onward. There was a slight breeze, but not enough to cool the skin hidden beneath layer after layer of linen, wool and outer leather strapping.

Soon, the target was seen by one of the men. Napoleon took out his spyglass, and extended it outward to see further. *Yes, this is the place.* He rode on, and ordered his men to follow and storm the gates. *Solar, schmolar*, Napoleon swore, *give me what you've got, I'll take you head on!*

After a few musket volleys aimed at the King's locks, they made it past the Gates. Shortly after, some men had collapsed during the Effort, falling off their horses, and covering their already swollen eyes. Their landing upon the sunny, sandy ground was just as oppressive against their shining woollen uniforms encapsulating them in the dreaded heat. The Weapon had, at last, been activated.

Napoleon got off his horse, willingly (*for a change*), and marched toward the main entrance. He knew the King and Queen were in residence, because he can see them looking down from their upstairs parlour rooms, giggling and smirking at him.

They pointed down at his men, knowing what havoc the former Louis' weapon had made on them. *Well, they shall giggle no more.* Napoleon gave the order and the soldiers charged toward the building.

The Royals had gone away from the window by now, as Napoleon and his troops were coming closer to the Palace. A further one hundred men had collapsed on the beige stone gravel. The forecourt was littered with men desperately trying to catch the stars Napoleon threw at them: the chance of glory to storm the Palace, overthrow the Royals and take their Place with Revolutionary Fervour.

Napoleon struggled on, not caring for the heat, and finishing off another canteen full of water, he barged himself upon the doors, splitting them wide open. He ran amok, and where the temperature knew no bounds, several more troops collapsed on the inside. *Merde.* He did not care. He felt alright, despite the heat, and kept on fighting to bring the Royal Family to *his* Justice.

Suddenly, a panic gripped the troops as they slowly broiled within their own suits. Many men could not take the Power of The Sun King and His Weapon. Many men died on the spot, gasping for air, or more likely, water. Napoleon grew weary and impatient with such wimps and promised himself he'd have a Grande Armée of his own. He did not give in to The Sun King's cruel beams and grabbed a drink from another canteen in his possession.

A prisoner-turned-soldier moaned, 'Monsieur, we cannot take much more of this Heat. It is appalling and most of us are dying from it.'

Napoleon hated wimps. *He hated whinging wimps even more.* 'What's a little heat got to do with it? We can handle this; for France, for Liberty, for Freedom. Fuck them, I'm going in.' He plunged toward his goal, with all the impatience of a just-fired bullet.

The soldier tried to keep up with his Master, but he, too, collapsed in the perishing beams of the Sun. One after another collapsed and no weapons were drawn. Not one. Napoleon expected the guards by now to defend the Palace, but everyone knew the Palace needed no defending. Everyone, *except Napoleon and his company.*

He realised the game was up and soon after, ordered a retreat. He may have been beaten today, but there will be much more time later. Over the next decade, he took his Revolutionary Passions abroad to other countries like Italy, for instance, and even had the nerve to go as far as Egypt. He was so obsessed with glory, he had this fervent desire to go to the Old Pyramids and have many men study the Vast Findings which lay within.

Unfortunately, The Sun King was not the only one to secure the Sun as a Weapon. The Egyptians had also used it long ago and their landscape made it perfect for such conditions. It was forbidding for any to go there *for the sake of it.* Napoleon would never storm an area for it's sake, *ever... but in this case, he did it anyway. He knew something lay beneath.* When the British found out, they had met Napoleon's Naval Fleet there. The resulting Battle of the Nile had given the commanding officer, Nelson, a head wound which led to a blinding in the right eye. That did not matter to him... *he won anyway.*

The resulting Ancient Discoveries gave mankind an opportunity to benefit from its history and the mysteries behind the ancient walls were no more. The French, meanwhile, had compiled tomes about the tombs and a lot of treasures were found. There was also a stone which featured several ancient texts upon it, the technical key to the path of old civilisations. It was formerly called the Loretta Stone, after an officer's wife, but the name changed later on to Rosetta, to honour the Englishwoman who would Defeat Napoleon.

Unfortunately, Napoleon was a greedy soul who wanted to Conquer the World. It upset Napoleon greatly that Britain was Master of the Seas, as whoever masters the seas has Dominance. He did not want a Dominant Britain. He decided to stage an Invasion and ordered his Fleet and Allies to engage the British.

Chapter XV

Nelson was the Admiral of the Fleet and a Great Seaman with one arm; the loss of his right arm, resulting from a battle in the Spanish islands. He was clever enough to learn to use his remaining left arm and in seeing past the eyelids. His mind was on his love for Emma Hamilton and in beating the Enemy at Sea.

He was a Seasoned Officer and took everything with a pinch of salt. He was original in his planning and strategy as well as treating his men with dignity, so everyone would look up to him as a Gracious Leader. There were many Admirals in the Fleet, but none of them matched the heroism, bravado and fame as Nelson.

Nelson was the son of a vicar down Norfolk way. Early on, he was eager and excited for worldly adventure. He entered Naval Service young (through familial connexion), and climbed the rigging, like everyone else, until he got up to his current Rank of Admiral. Nelson was the one who wanted to win the Battle; the War would be won by Someone Else.

He sighted the Enemy of a combined French and Spanish ships bottlenecked at Cadiz in Spain and gave out a flagged signal, 'England Expects Every Man Will Do His Duty'. Once the Enemy broke the blockade against them, they went after Nelson and his fleet of thirty-two ships near the Cape of Trafalgar. On 21 October 1805, The British fleet sailed into the Enemy Fleet and giving them broadsides where no side had been broaded before. Nelson wanted to reach out and touch them, very badly, so they could no longer bob afloat and invade the British coast.

The ships were firing on both sides and masts and sails had shattered, split and fell on the helpless men who thought they were doing their duty. Nelson soon ascended on deck and kissed Captain Hardy for luck. Hardy blushed and carried on helping the gunmen and crew. The air was thick with wooden pieces, which splintered all over the side of the Victory, as enemy cannon fire pulverised the crew.

A Midshipman, Joshua Compton, fell from a splintered plank of wood in the leg. He was a few feet away from Nelson, who immediately rushed to help the lad. (Nelson was particular about Midshipmen and felt they needed guidance and example. He had admiration for them in their hopeful careers in the Navy, as he recalled his suckling years... now a lifetime ago.)

When Nelson bent down to help the Midshipman, he had narrowly missed a French sniper's bullet that could have been meant for him. The bullet boomeranged against a metallic piece on the mast and hit a nearby crewman. As he removed his badge laden overcoat to cover the Midshipman, Nelson spat out a curse when that crewman's blood hit and soaked the white surface of his waistcoat, through to the inner shift. Nelson put his outer coat inside out; although the pieces of honour would be uncomfortable to lean against, *the inner odour of the lining itself would kill the poor child instantly*. He needed to give him a chance.

Nelson called out, 'Ugh!', out of frustration. Then, he had the lad sent below deck to the surgeon, who Nelson hoped would help Midshipman Compton. Another crewman assisted in carrying the lad and Nelson followed them both, the celebrated coat still covering the injured.

A voice called from the darkness, 'I trust all goes well, Admiral?'

Nelson recognised the Surgeon, William Beatty, who just finished working on another crewman. 'Yes, but Compton's copped it. I've just been hit by blood.'

'Not your own, I presume,' Beatty said, covering the body he examined, then inspected the blood on Nelson, 'I do not see any open wound or torn clothing.'

'No. There are no cuts; the fabric's intact. Still, we will have to burn it, I suppose. Plenty more where that came from,' Nelson laughed, then continued, 'Can you help the boy?'

Beatty had his previous patient taken to where the other deceased were put and Nelson discreetly removed the outer coat, inside out still, and threw it aside. The Midshipman was laid out on a table and the surgeon checked the wound. That bit of plank was still lodged in his leg area, where it festered like the French trying to take over the World.

'The wood's stuck in there pretty good. I believe the leg would have to be removed, but as it had been there for some time, I can see an infection starting. The wood itself had a fair distance and there is detritus on it, which could have entered the child's system. In any case, even if we took the leg, there is predicting a minimal survival rate for him.' Beatty did not pour out much hope here.

Compton stirred, feverish and delirious. He gripped the Admiral's left arm and stared at him for a few seconds.

'Kismet,' he said to Nelson.

'Kismet,' the Admiral repeated, whilst the boy lost the grip and died.

Nelson's eyes started to water, as he was well miffed at all around him. Maybe it should have been *him* that died, and not a young lad, just starting out on his first run. The Admiral had been around the seas for much of his life and got a good sense of learning and wisdom from being at sea, especially in War. He knew he was needed in Warfare and he played a vital role. Yet, he felt he was 'past it' and other men, like Compton, needed to take his place... *in time*.

Then, Nelson wept.

Bitterly.

Like he's never wept before.

Hardy had come down from the upper deck and showed concern.

Nelson turned to him, embracing his Captain, and cried, 'Kismet, Hardy!'

'Oh, no, not again,' Hardy moaned.

The Admiral composed himself through the tears, 'No, Hardy, it's Arabic, meaning Fate.'

'Ah, that's good then. I thought you'd gone off Emma for me.'

'I would never go off Emma, but I am very fond of you. You are all my Band of Brothers.'

'You're giving me the Nelson Touch, Sir.'

'Oh, sorry about that,' Nelson shrunk back, embarrassed.

'I came down to tell you the French and Spanish fleets have scattered; they're practically destroyed.'

'Good, good... and what of our Ships?'

'None lost, but the Enemy lost most of theirs.'

Nelson nodded weakly, too numb to venture forth.

Hardy gripped his Arm, and smiled, 'We've won, sir.'

The Admiral stood stone faced, as if trying to see the big picture from a column. 'So we have. Gather up the remnants and return to Blighty with the News.'

'I will write up notices straightaway,' Hardy volunteered.

* * * * * *

Back in England, Nelson, with his fellow Officers and Staff, met The King who gave them commendations, and a Thanksgiving Service was held at St. Paul's. It was a service to remember the Fallen as well as the Heroes. Nelson gave a Dramatic Speech to Honour those who Served with Him and for Him. He told those present about Midshipman Compton and how he tried to help him. He spoke of the Endless Flying Debris, the Lung-Filling Smoke, and the Cursing of the Enemy. This was the Enemy's Defeat which prevented the Napoleonic Invasion of Britain.

As further reward, The King gave Nelson mastery over the budding Canal System. He was posted as Commander of His Majesty's Canals, continuing his Career at Sea, but protecting Interests at Home. He would live on a Canal Barge with Emma and their daughter Horatia, to monitor the trades and industries using the System.

* * * * * *

Meanwhile, Totteringstate Hall bore witness to our growing brood. Cynthia Rose was so much like her mother and curious for the intellectual.

In addition to domestic learning from Fantasie and Daffnette (when my Cynthia was away to serve The King), she always read from the Library. Amongst our collection, there were books relating to religion, history, music, art, and Literature, including Shakespeare (*who would not want to boast about that!?*), to name a few.

As for my other children, Cedric followed me into soldiering and enlisted in the old Totteringstate Regiment I once served in, and presently active in the local militia. Mary Emma followed Cynthia Rose's taste for the intellect and decided to be a teacher, helping Lottie and Daffnette in the village school. Leslie did not care for village life at all and found his way toward the London stage to become an actor. *Well, I did say we were an unusual lot!*

My dear wife, the former colonist, Cynthia remained in her position with The King on and off, taking breaks to visit the family (something His Majesty would definitely relate to!). She told us of The King's Interest in meeting Cynthia Rose and the result was an appointment with His Majesty. In due course, Cynthia Rose met George III at the usual place, St. James. They went for a meal together at another location at Kew, where it was more intimate. *I think they got on well.*

I long since retired from the Army and spent most of my days at the Hall. My other military friends finally went on to other Assignments. Tarleton went to Ireland, Rawdon was posted to India and Simcoe founded the Upper Canada Region for the British Crown. Meanwhile, Buckingham, Nay-Smith and Cateliffe had been on other postings. Lottie was still in charge of the Parish and Daffnette helped out where ever she was needed. I knew they would be better suited for one another. Fantasie and Mr Amos had married and I, in my crazy way, decided to free them, not too long after.

They were now no longer our property but our *employees*, should they have wished it. As they had a small family of their own, they decided to remain and serve. This time, however, we gave them a reasonable wage for their work.

I was more happier with Cynthia, with whom I spent time with during her time away from the Court. We went away together, just us, to Sydmouth for our little break away. We enjoyed every moment of it, walking along the lanes, looking in shoppes, even attending the local church, if a Sunday was included. I caught up with Greyrivers and my sister Emmadayle. I also had more relations with Cynthia, as we reciprocated honour in our private sectors. Our ages seemed against us by now, but we did not care. The sun yielded to a faded kiss, as I nibbled on her tender mass. I remained in love with her and she was a good wife to me. It made me think about the time I was reserved for Daffnette, but I was grateful *to challenge the reservation.*

Upon our return home, Cynthia suddenly developed a fever and had not lasted too long. When she died a few days later, it broke my heart terribly, especially as I did not understand why my sweet love had been taken from me. *We have been through so much together*; it was most Distasteful of Fate to Lead such an Insurrection. I was so certain her constitution was strong, as was her mind, and wilfully intact, 'til the end. Alas, Death always has the Final Say. I cried and cried for days, inconsolable.

She was buried at Totteringstate Parish and I ordered a Grand Mausoleum to be made in Her Honour. She was a true Woodes-Hastings, and I will make Eternity know it, *despite her unacceptable upbringing!* At the funeral, Lottie presided over the service and spoke of her courage, adaptability and love. He knew she had a difficult beginning and did not include the disgrace in his eulogy. *He knew better...*

Everyone else just thought she was a rugged old colonist returning to England, having served The King in Staying the Rebellion in Colonies. Alright, she was not 'old' as such, but she definitely had a liveliness and maturity about her that was noticeable in the early days... *before she mellowed and let go.*

Everyone in the village and beyond paid their respects to Cynthia, even my old Army mates who were with us during her rescue from the Colonies. No one discussed the oddities she had, nor did they enquire in regards to her old family. *We saw to that!* She was remembered for her strength and no-nonsense attitude.

On a rare appearance outside the Royal scope, The King and a favoured servant, Lantin, had attended, too. The King felt a loss just as great as when he lost his youngest male children so many years before... *Cynthia meant so much to Him.* She kept Him Stable during some rough times, especially furthering the Security of the North American Colonies. He wept grievously, nearly going mad, for fear of losing a grip on Reality, letting go the Realm of State and being made a fool of by France.

As this was no time for a formal audience, Cynthia Rose approached The King with concern.

'Your Majesty,' she said, curtsying. She then got up and reached out toward Him.

'Cynthia the Younger, I presume,' The King responded, 'I remember our prior meeting.'

'Many call me Cynthia Rose, or Rose... As you'd like it.'

The King's mood changed, 'Shakespeare fan?'

'I've read his plays. I figured the phrase would lighten the air.'

'Indeed it did,' He hesitated to think, 'Erm, I know this would seem sudden, but there is now a Vacancy in my Court. Would you like to fill it?'

Cynthia Rose was astounded, 'Me? Gosh! You are asking me to fill my mother's shoes?'

The King blushed, eyes fully dried, 'Well, not that they would fit you; she did have small feet.'

She smiled. 'I know what you mean, Sir, and I would be happy to assist You.' *The opportunity for a Woodes-Hastings to serve The King was never far away.*

'Splendid!' The King gave Cynthia Rose a cuddle.

I was chatting to an old friend of mine when I saw The King and my eldest in a firm embrace. I trusted she had agreed to continue her mother's role as The King's Minder. I walked up to them and bowed to The King.

'No need, no need, Willec,' He said.

'Why, thank you.'

'You had lost someone special. I do not expect the red carpet here. 'Tis Cynthia's Day, not Mine.'

'You are too kind.'

The King took his Leave and I walked alongside my eldest daughter.

'I must congratulate you on your appointment, my girl. All your good learning will be put to test and you will no longer be living secluded in the Hall.'

'That is alright, Father, I know what I am doing. I've prepared myself through reading and exploring. I will serve His Majesty, just as Mother did.'

'Good lass,' I commended, turning to face her as I put my hand on her chin, cupping it. *She looks so much like the wife... Beautiful.*

Most of the funeral party went separate ways and it was now Cynthia Rose's turn to attend the Court. I was amazed on how she grew, and with goodly influences on her. I wanted to spend more time with my Rose before she left.

* * * * * *

Cynthia Rose and George III got on very well and much time was spent away from us at Totteringstate. The King, during this period, had lost another child, the youngest, Amelia and He was distraught. It was Cynthia Rose's job to keep Him composed and in order. She was soothing and had done a fine job in stabilising The King's Moods. It takes much to be with someone in need and a little care does go a long way.

They sat at the window seat in one of the many rooms at Kew Palace. The sun was shining, showing off the modest-looking decor inside. There was taste, but it was comfortable, not lavish. Homely, but not too plain.

Cynthia Rose asked, 'Do you want to take a stroll outside?'

The King, still with tears in his eyes, agreed, 'It might take my mind off things. It is good you are here, Miss Rose.'

'Glad to serve,' she curtsied.

'You know you do not have to do that!'

She smiled at him. He giggled a little, but cleared his throat. They walked in the afternoon sun.

'You know you remind me so much of her... you are so like her, what what,' He rambled.

'I am flattered you think that way about me, but remember I am not her. I can never substitute for anyone.'

'Yes, yes, I know,' George waved impatiently, 'But, as I am dwindling in twilight, I like to imagine, if I may.'

'Just remember, I am Cynthia Rose, your Minder. I know you are in your Twilight.'

'And what a Twilight it is, eh??' He winked at her.

She carried on walking. George tried to keep up. She turned around and quickly slowed the pace.

'I thought a good run would do you good.'

'Ah, 'tis difficult to keep, to keep up, what??! Slow down, girl, I need to talk.'

They found a bench and sat down. Cynthia Rose looked into The King's wide saucer shaped blue eyes.

'What do you need to discuss?'

George stared at the tree for a good minute. 'Do you have anyone special in your life?'

'Not that I am aware of... I have been at my studies and helping out at home. Why do you ask?'

The King revealed a conniving nature about him that was very out of character. 'My son, the Prince of Wales, has a fellow in his Service by the name of Elderfynne. He's a servant... a dishy servant. You'd like him, eh eh???'

'Elderfynne?'

'Yes. He is a few years older than you and spent many years with my son. I think you will like him. They say he is very delightful and could be a good match to your intelligence.'

Cynthia Rose was astounded a Royal Person was trying to match make for her. She played along with it... *I will judge when I meet the fellow.*

The King blushed but did not flinch. He kept still about it, 'Actually, I just decided, yes, you need someone. I am sending you on a mission. You are to work for my son, who is floundering at the moment. He is deep in debt, eats to much and holds parties on the waterfront, as if it were *everybody's* business. I need you to rein him in, yeah? If you manage to keep the old fellow in Order, than your reward can be Elderfynne. What do you say?'

'We've just got to know each other and now you are sending me away!'

'No, no, no, do not think that. Truly, I can manage. I do not need keeping in line, actually, even though my balance much of the time is off. Hey Hey!'

'So you believe you no longer need my care?'

'Well, I will keep you for some time longer, whilst the arrangements of transfer are commenced. You stay with me, then when the Prince calls you, you go!' Then, George rubbed his stubbly jaw. 'How do you like it?'

'Sir?'

'The stubble. I'm trying to grow it out.'

'Why?'

'To baffle people, why why not not?'

Cynthia Rose laughed, 'You are the type of Monarch that keeps one on one's toes, aren't you?!'

The King let go and scoffed, 'Eah, go on! I can manage. I have servants but I prefer you and your Mother's company best of all. I am not as bad off as some think I am. I firmly feel I am no longer Mad. Damn the doctors!'

He was becoming sly in his older age. The company He kept was doing a world of good for him, almost to the point of self-sufficiency again... despite that stubble which will eventually grow into a full-length wizard-style beard, after Cynthia Rose departed his Company.

'I would not think of you as Mad, Sire. It is not noticeable to me.'

'It is not obvious to others, either. Well, it takes one to know one, what what! My son is set up in Brighton and built a crazy Palace there. He enjoys the comforts of the Region. I'm more a Weymouth boy, myself.'

'Tastes differ, then?'

'Why, yes they do. I will have a letter of introduction, for formal purposes only, for I know His Highness would surely recognise you. You will serve him as you did myself and you will save him from himself. He's a Right Rag and about to become a King someday. He needs guidance.'

'I think that would be the last thing he needs, Your Majesty, from what I heard. I trust you do not get on well together.'

'We have our differences, as you pointed out earlier. You can steady him on. I can no longer help him. He does not want my help.'

Cynthia Rose paused. 'Can I return to Totteringstate first for a quick visit with family?'

'Of course you can. There is no rush. True, I am not getting any younger, but I have faith I will still be around and not cause a Constitutional Crisis. You may have your time.'

The sun began to set and the Pair returned inside for dinner.

Chapter XVI

The years had gained up on me as I was getting older and slightly infirm. My Cynthia Rose had come home from her time with The King. She sat in the parlour with me whilst I was playing a card game called Patience.

'His Majesty wants me to cater to The Prince in Brighton,' she explained.

I was impressed, but worried. 'This is sudden.'

'The King and I spent much time together and He felt His son needs to be dealt with. He is getting out of control of himself and, get this, The King is trying to match me up with some servant of his called Elderfynne.'

Elderfynne? *Ah, yes... I had forgotten about that offshoot of our family... hmm...* this would not be incest as such; the link had veered away for centuries without a rematch into our own lineage. *May do the lass some good.*

'It sounds like The Royals are concerned for your welfare, my dear girl. You are young, but not getting any younger. 'Tis about time you had settled down with someone.'

I paused and realised a flashback... *now, where have I heard THAT before?* I sniggered to myself within the folds of my card deck.

'Father, I'm all for it and I know to work hard getting The Prince in Order, so he may be an effective King someday. I heard his Affairs are in disarray, mismatched and chaotic. I am also wondering why you had not been pushing a romance upon me instead of someone, like The King of England??!'

I answered, with soothing calmness in my voice, 'My girl. My darling growing girl, I would not ever tell you who to marry, but I would like to see you married, one day. When you are ready to do so, you settle in with someone you *LOVE*. Ah, your mother would have been very proud of you, serving Royalty, and for even them helping you with a bit of romance.'

'Did it take much to woo Mother?'

'No, we got together in the most awkward way... ,' I then shared the Indian Raid experience with Cynthia Rose, as well as the State House Raid, the Battle of Lorne Bridge (where I had been wounded) and the return journey to England. *Such fond memories for me...* and a history lesson for the Rose.

She listened carefully, nodding and taking it all in. I tried not to divulge the controversial side, yet I felt it was necessary to share some of it. I pointed out her mother had a non-Christian upbringing which was abusive and soul destroying. Once we got her out of the mess that family put her into, she was willing to begin a proper Christian life.

'So you're saying that family coerced Mother into their faith?'

'Yes, Cynthia Rose, they did... and it was not pleasant. They were not even of that faith to begin with! They were recent converts who snuck in, so-to-speak. Sharp minds, but sharp tongues and a quick hand, too, no doubt... I had not witnessed that bit, yet it would not surprise me if they did use physical force to back up the principle.'

'Gosh,' she said, 'But I am not a part of them, right?'

'No, you are not. That family belonged to Cynthia's mother. They adopted her after the mother had died.'

'What from?'

'Oh, I believe it was epilepsy, or some convulsive malady.'

'Sounds like they themselves were convulsive!'

'Now, Rose, don't be too harsh. They did what they did and we got her out and disconnected her from everything to do with them using legal means. You have no connexion to that family, in any way, shape or form, other than you are at least a *mere fraction* of them.'

'Why a fraction?'

'Her father was Italian. He died in the streets of New York, after he was given an ultimatum from that family, to convert to their ways. He refused and paid the price. He lost his wife and his daughter, who was Cynthia. He turned to the bottle and languished in the streets 'til he died.'

'Did Mother and her father ever meet?'

I gave the heaviest sigh as the burden was being lifted from my soul. 'No, they never did.'

'Poor Mother,' Cynthia Rose lamented. She began to cry and I gave her a hug.

'Now my love, you will be strong for me. You are the Elder Rose and you must follow the path open to you. That family has nothing to do with you, and, happily, you have nothing to do with them. As all the members therein are deceased, they are of no consequence to you.

'You are English and a Woodes-Hastings. Your maternal line of Italian-Germanic is irrelevant for the long run. You were raised at Totteringstate to think for yourself and to choose what you want to do with yourself and your life. You are well read, inquisitive and of a good sound mind. *Your mind is your own.* You take what Life offers you. If it offers this Elderfynne chappie, well, go for it... for you will not get another chance. And what's more, he is Royally Approved and if the Royal Family has a hand in the match, then how bad could it be?'

'I must decide that for myself, Father,' she said sheepishly.

'You do that... and hell, you might find him invigorating for yourself.'

An invigorating fellow, she thought... *I know they are not pushing this, but...*

'I feel good we took time for this conversation; it gives me more time with you.' She kissed me on the cheek and gave me a long cuddle.

'I thought it would do you good, my Rose,' I soothed... *and it soothed me I had this conversation with her, as I'd hoped.*

A few weeks went by as Cynthia Rose was preparing to leave for her appointment in Brighton. I, of course, had to secure my estate, as I was feeling the life I once had, ebb away and fast. Time just started to become slower, then sluggish, then... I was soon confined to bed. Cynthia Rose remained for the time, just in case she was needed by me. I did not want to keep her here, as I know a Royal Appointment must always be kept.

'I'll write a quick note of dispatch to the Prince. I am sure he'll understand,' she commented.

She got Mr Amos's son, John, to deliver the letter. Thankfully, Totteringstate was not too far from Brighton.

The Prince answered the message a week later. *'Take your time. I can wait... and will live and dine as lavishly as no other... until you are received here. HRH '*

Ha-ha, Cynthia Rose mocked. *That Prince will be a handful.* Still, it may be fun to work with him, but for the moment, she was needed at home.

I was going in and out of consciousness, as I tried to do daily tasks. Things were not looking good for me and the Rose had to endure my convalescence... *or was it illness?* I honestly was unsure and at this point, who cared?

One morning, as the sun streamed into my bedroom, I had woken up in my double sized bed. I reached for my Cynthia, but she was not there (*damn, I forgot!*). The Rose was running around, doing errands and helping about. I suddenly felt faint and, and... the weakened state o'ercame my soul and fight. I, I... tried to get up to enter the tedium of the day...

And then the world stopped around me.

PART II

Cynthia Rose Woodes-Hastings

Chapter XVII

It had been some time since Father's death. I was still reeling from its Dance. He'd gotten a good send-off, his surviving twin Lottie presiding over the arrangements and ceremonial aspects. Unfortunately, many of Father's friends had passed away by now or served on Assignments abroad. I hardly knew any of them and Father never really told me much, other than that final tête-à-tête we had just before he died. Then, at last, he opened up to me and saw to it that I knew more about my mother's history, *as rubbish as it was.* Although I understood it was someone else's life and there was no point in trying to make it one's own, it was interesting to see what happened to Mother before she met Father.

Whilst the servants were working away in the household, Lottie and I saw to going over various papers. Daffnette, his wife, recently passed away, leaving no living children. My brothers and sister attended the funeral, but moved on afterward to their own lives. I spent more time at Totteringstate than any of them; *I guess I cared... I was the eldest.*

'I remember these... the paperwork concerning your mother,' Lottie informed me, 'I believe they are now yours. You may do with them as you wish.'

He gave me what seemed like a ream of paper. I read through them and realised *they meant nothing to me.* What's more, they were from another country, and not even a country, but a *colony.* Gosh! All I had was a christening record, kept at Totteringstate Parish Church, which, if anyone cared to look, was available for viewing (by appointment only, of course). I could not believe the history of this woman... my... my mother... this was madness. More madder than my Royal Friend, The King, who seemed far more Stable than this. *No wonder He'd let me go!*

I looked at Lottie. 'Do I have to keep this lot?'

'Why, do you have other intentions? We could put it away in our familial archives.'

'Nah, where's the nearest fireplace?'

'You plan to burn the lot?' Lottie's blue eyes bulged open.

'Well... what would I do with it? So she came from New York. I see she'd changed her name; had an early Baptism which someone else tried to expunge but failed. She was adopted, got married... well, that marriage bit should be kept at least,' I decided.

"Tis your decision my Rose,' Lottie consented.

'I know and understand she had a complicated life before Father came along. I also have a funny suspicion Mother would agree with me in not wanting to retain these *incriminating* records.'

Lottie looked up at me, and said, 'It was complicated... very! Your mother Cynthia, was controlled by an *overzealous grandmother*, I heard, who took over her raising. This person tried to gauge every part of Cynthia's life, much to Cynthia's Detriment. Her emotional state was very volatile when she first came here. As time went by and during her appointment with The King, she mellowed considerably. But, your mother definitely loved Willec. I trust he told you he was supposed to marry another?'

'No, but I can only guess... Daffnette?'

'Aye,' Lottie expressed in sadness, missing her already, 'I opted to marry Daff to shut up our Father. Willec was concerned about the upcoming Colonial conflict and needed to be available when he got called up. He was an exceptional Soldier and someone to be proud of.'

'I know, Uncle.' My mind was gassed with so much cloud cover of thought, it was not funny. I could not wait to depart for Brighton to serve His Highness. I had one more question to ask.

'Do you know anything about someone in the Prince's service called Elderfynne? I am to meet this fellow once I am in the Prince's Court. The King told me he was 'a dishy servant'.'

Lottie sighed. Another sliver of family history was revealed to me.

'Elderfynne is a very distant cousin... from an illegitimate lineage created several hundred years ago,' he confirmed, staring straight at me.

I panicked, 'This is not incest, is it?'

'No,' Lottie stated, 'He is a relation, through a common ancestor, but the lineage had not crossed into our own, as of yet.'

'Wow,' I was awestruck. I realised if I connect with this Elderfynne, the lineage would meet again... but as there was many centuries between our families, *it should be safe to court him... or for him to court me.*

True, I was unmarried and not getting younger. I firmly believed I looked alright, but I did not wish to put myself in the running. I also had an Appointment to attend.

I weeded out my parent's Marriage Certificate, then I took the rest of the paperwork to the nearest fireplace and threw the lot in. At least I have proof of my Legitimacy... *no one will ever call Me a bastard!* I was told what I was made of and *it was all good!*

I left the room and a few days hence, I made my way to Brighton by carriage.

* * * * *

Brighton, originally called 'Brighthelmstone', was a little village settled for agriculture and fishing purposes. As it was by the sea, that made perfect sense... *a perfect seaside town with a Prince in residence.* There was a Pier as well as many symmetrically lined homes looking out toward the sea. *Ah yes, and the odd piece the Prince built... The Royal Pavilion*, which everybody who did not fancy the exotic architecture, had put down as an eyesore. I personally thought it was beautiful, if not a reasonable depiction of places one never had visited before. If it was of the mind, it was of nothing but pure genius. The Prince wanted to make a statement that he was unlike his Father in many ways, especially in taste. Outwardly, I think The King would hate this place, though secretly, *He would have to admire the cheek of it all.*

I stepped out of the carriage and a valet awaited me by the doorway of the Pavilion.

'His Highness is expecting you,' he said.

'I know, sir,' I replied.

'He told me he was looking forward to your working with him.'

'Oh, is he now?' I quipped.

We walked into a waiting area, full of wallpapered chinoisery. It was busy on the eyes, and sometimes it was difficult to see its story through, as the pieces kept repeating themselves in pattern. *Still, this is the Prince's Palace...*

'Wait here,' the valet ordered, walking out.

I sat down on one of the chairs with dragon arms and lions at the legs. It was a few minutes, so I took out a book I brought with me and read.

Suddenly, I heard footsteps approach. I put the book away and sat upright. The Prince, and that valet I saw earlier, stood by the door. The Prince entered and I got up to curtsey.

'Your Highness,' I declared.

'Oh no, we will have none of that. That might have been good for Papa, but you are not working for Him!' The Prince sounded agitated.

'Forgive the courtesy. But, I thought,' I explained.

'You thought what?' The Prince's blue eyes peered right down to my soul.

'I, I...,' I began to stutter in his Presence.

'You should have gotten used to being in Royal Circles. Yes, we do have to keep a precedence here, too, but as you are working among us, the formalities are unnecessary.'

I stood upright, 'I see, sir.'

'Well, as we get to know one another, we will drop the 'sir' nonsense, too.'

'At least you do not go, 'what what!',' I noticed.

'No, I am not His Majesty and I am not mad like Him,' the Prince retorted.

'He is not Mad. He told me so, that is why I am here.'

'Oh yes, now what was it he said, *'to save me'*, by some chance?'

'That is what I was told and to meet this Elderfynne fellow.'

'You have already seen him,' His Highness snickered teasingly.

'WHAT??!' *I thought the fellow looked a bit like...*

'Let me put you out of your Godforsaken misery,' he called, 'Wickett!'

The valet re-entered the room. 'You need me, then?'

'Wickett, this is my new Minder, fresh from Kew and Totteringstate, Cynthia Rose Woodes-Hastings. Cynthia Rose, this is John Pickwick Elderfynne.'

Elderfynne held out his hand, 'How do you do, Miss Rose... may I call you that? Woodes-Hastings is a bit of a mouthful.'

'Yes, yes, that it is,' the Prince exhaled in haste, turning to me, 'That alright with you?'

I answered, 'Yes', then I paused, looking at Mr Elderfynne with keen interest.

Elderfynne looked concerned, 'Is there something amiss?'

I began to stutter with emotions I had never ever felt before, 'You look, ah... like...'

The realisation came... FATHER!!!!!!!!!

I clumsily blurted out, 'You look exactly like Father!'

'Yes, I admit I do look a bit like your father. I had a suspicion there would be interest in me, due to that side of things. You must have loved him very much and miss him with equal melancholy.'

'I... I did, Mr Elderfynne.'

'Alright now, that's enough. Wickett, you go back to your duties. Cynthia Rose, you're with me,' the Prince commanded, 'Let's go. '

I left the room with His Highness, with Mr Elderfynne watching past us. He was a tall gentleman, well suited, with a neatness about him. His hair had a slight curl at the ends with waves forming the body, and his face, well, was just like Father's. *It was a challenge to get used to this; after all, I've just had Father buried!*

The Prince led me through some seriously loud corridors where the chintz of his passion screamed through every pore on the walls. The sideboards had little Chinese nick-nacks of porcelain ranging from vases to figurines. I also saw something that (I believed) looked like a salt cellar shaped like a merman holding a huge trident. It was truly astounding... the look and cheek of this place and it would take such a Prince to see to it all.

'Ah, here we are,' His Highness stated, opening the door to another screaming chintz-filled room. *What had The King been thinking by sending me here?* The poor fellow *must* have been mad. Even He would not take such a burden on. *I bet Mother would have loved it.*

We entered the Royal Apartment suite which included the bedroom. He beckoned me toward the bed and had me sit down for a chat.

'So, now that you are here, what are your plans, hmmm? How do you plan to mind me?' The Prince waited for my answer with bated breath.

'I thought I'd...,' I tried to speak but was quickly cut off.

'You, Miss Rose, must be famished. I'll order something from the kitchen for you.' The Prince grabbed the pull cord to ring for attention.

Moments later, Mr Elderfynne stood at the door. 'Yes, Your Highness?'

'Wickett, get me the finest you have from the kitchen.'

'Certainly, would that be the full Carême-sized meal or a small one for you and Miss Rose?'

'I'm not too picky...,' the Prince turned to me, 'Cynthia Rose?'

'I'll take the small size. Trying to watch the weight here,' I confessed.

'You look splendid, Miss Rose,' Mr Elderfynne complimented. 'I'll get two medium-sized orders for you.' He left to retrieve the food.

The Prince sighed, 'Now, where were we?'

'You wanted to know what I would do to help sort you out. Well, for one thing, you need to stop the frivolous banqueting and spending.'

The Prince was flabbergasted, 'What?! And disappoint my audiences??'

'You'll disappoint them more when you've heard my idea, if you continue to have your so-called banquets.'

'Oh yeah?' The Prince crossed his arms and the blue eyes focused strangely upon my person.

'Give the leftovers to the local poor.'

'You must be joking... you're even madder than Papa!'

'No, I am not... it is about time you gave back to the community. Let the locals have a taste of the high life.'

'And gob on my lawns? No thank you, ma'am!'

'It's an idea... or how about trimming your events down to a reasonable size, then?'

'I'd like to trim YOU to a reasonable size... but you are beneath me and one mustn't do such things.'

I shouted, 'I am a Woodes-Hastings and, mind you, it never stopped *you* from going after other women!'

'Oooh, you feisty little one... No, I will not touch you.'

'Why? Am I not good enough? Too tall, too cute, too intelligent?'

'Too virginal. I'm trying to save YOU, my girl.'

'Save ME? From what, your familial madness?'

'No, for Elderfynne... You see, I am not a Bad Prince, as everybody wishes to think, my pretty,' the Prince said.

'Why are you and The King trying to hook me up with Mr Elderfynne?'

'Because, my dear,' the Prince admitted, 'I know you are unmarried and not getting any younger, and it would be a shame to waste your beauty on the riff-raff of society, including the ones in higher circles, if you get my meaning.'

'I do understand,' I replied.

'The other reason is... we Royals believe he would be an excellent match for you.'

'Do you know he is related to me?'

'Yes, but only from a distant ancestor, not in recent times. So, there you have it.'

'Has it been a Royal Hobby to find suitors for others?'

'Only if it suits us... and we do want to help you, Miss Rose. Well, what... after what your mother accomplished for us, I mean, it is the least we could do for you. She served us nicely, helping Papa on an even keel. You've carried on the Service. It's also part of the Madness. Papa thinks he could make people happy by matching them up in love. He tried that on with one of my sisters and got her engaged to a Mr Elm.'

'Was Mr Elm beneath her, by some chance?'

'Oh, of course, but if it is with The King's Blessing, then it is alright. Anyway, we later found that this Mr Elm was a tree in the gardens of Kew Palace. I had to have it cut down to discourage Papa from continuing with the arrangement.

'Naturally, He had forgotten about it, but my sister never did and cried herself to sleep. It upset Mama greatly.'

'I bet it had,' I mocked, but realised how bad the Madness had gone since I'd left Him. He was so certain that He was able to cope and work on his Issues, but then, He had another relapse. The Family did not resort to violent methods, as The King had not lashed out at anyone. He stayed quiet in His room and amused Himself.

My face revealed a grimace which the Prince noticed acutely, 'Do not worry about The King, Miss Rose. He turned you over to me.'

'But he is now not of sound mind,' I argued.

'Yes, but at the time of the turnover, He was,' the Prince went to his convenience table to pour some claret and offered to me.

'Want some?'

'Yeah, why not?'

He poured two glasses, giving one to me and taking a sip of his. A knock came to the door and Elderfynne had brought in a full tray filled with a whole cooked pheasant, quails eggs, slices of ham, a rich sweet bread, and puddings with sultanas, nuts, chocolat, and whatnot, covered with the sweetest marzipans on this side of the Atlantic (because I've heard the sugar came from the *other* side).

'You may go now Wickett,' the Prince turned to me, 'Do tuck in, lass, tuck in. So, what do you think of the Palace?'

I started eating, looking around. 'It is exceptional, sir.'

'Your mother had a problem with that.'

'With what?'

'The 'sir' business.'

'So what does one call a Prince? Do you have a nickname? Do you want to be called George, like your father?'

'I am nothing like Him!'

'That is obvious,' I swallowed a bit of meat, still looking around. I took a quick sip of the claret.

'Well, duh, Papa is a boring sod compared to ME!'

'His Taste was Modest, sir,' I calmly said, trying to wind him up, just cos he teased me earlier.

'For Modest, read BORING!' The Prince protested.

I took a bite of one of the cakes... 'Umm, this is very tasty.'

'Coconut flavouring.'

'Coconauts...,' I pondered, 'I wonder if they would go up into outer space?'

'No, they fly o'er their nests, far away... you've been reading Voltaire... you're just as nuts as Papa.'

'It is a good story... in perspective.'

'Ha-ha,' the Prince joked on.

'When will I have time with Mr Elderfynne?'

'Why, you want a day off already?'

'No, I want to see why you lot want me with him.'

'We will see, lass.'

I let out a sound of disappointment.

'You'll get there...,' he looked at me, 'And you may call me Prinny.'

* * * * * *

The King, had been living at Kew Palace during his later years. He sat in his room daily, playing on a harpsichord the music of Handel, his favourite composer. The problem was His eyesight was dimming and He could not read the music anymore. However, He loved the melodies, playing on as if there was nothing wrong, much to everyone's dismay. When he started singing the choruses, other family members and household staff found it just a bit too disturbing. Eventually, they politely told him to keep the noise down. It was worse when He wanted to have some of them participate in the singing!

'It's such a pity Cynthia Rose isn't here,' one of the Royal daughters, Sophia sighed.

Another one of the daughters, Mary, joined in, 'Agreed, sister; she would have had him in rein. He has got No Direction now.'

'Nay, he has One Direction... the Direction toward Oblivion.'

'I hate to see Papa like this. Oh, I wish we were like our brothers so we could do Something in this world.'

'I hate this confinement. 'Tis like a nunnery, this is!' Sophia's frustration was self-evident.

'Concurred, sister... so what do we do about Papa?'

'Guess we have to resort to humouring him and try to use the same tactics Miss Rose used. It should be easy, as we ARE... His... dear daughters.'

Sophia and Mary walked through the corridor to join their Papa when a letter was taken to them by Lantin, The King's Favourite Servant, on one of the many silver plated platters used for such purpose.

'For The King,' he said.

'Likewise,' Mary replied, taking the letter from him. She looked at the front. 'This is for Papa... I wonder if he could comprehend this sort of thing.'

'Let's try it out, shall we?' Sophia giggled, desperately trying to make the situation lighter.

'Yea, let's go,' Mary darted away.

She ran across the Hallway when a vocal din was heard. She and Sophia followed the sound to a door and opened it straightaway without thinking. The resounding chords echoed into the Hallway as The King stopped playing to see who entered his sanctuary.

'Now, who do we have here?' The King reached out... 'Oh, is it Amelia? *No, no, can't be, she's dead...* Could it be the Princess Charlotte? *Oh yeah, she moved to Germany.* Who's there, then?'

The two Princesses snickered outrageously, saying together, ''Tis us, Papa, Sophia and Mary!'

'Ah, my beautiful girls,' He got up, carefully, to give them a hug, 'To what do I owe this Pleasure?'

Mary took the letter out of her inner petticoat pocket. 'This came for you,' she said.

'For me? Now, who would be sending me a fan letter, I wonder,' He chuckled, knowing most of Government policy was no longer His concern and most of the People forgot about Him and concentrated on the Prince in Brighton.

'I do not know, Papa, I did not read it,' Mary stated.

'Didn't think you would... but, as my eyesight's a bit duff, could you do us a kindness and read this for me, please, old girl? You may sit on the chair.'

'I will, Papa,' Mary sat down with Sophia next to her, broke the seal and began to read aloud:

'From His Majesty's Forces in Europe to King George III of Great Britain—
SIR:
We've done a sneak attack on the Enemy. We routed and then captured Napoleon near the town of Waterloo where he surrendered to us. We took him with no causalities on either side. The Enemy did not even bother engaging us! What can be done with him?
Your Humble Servant,
Wellington.'

The King looked up. 'Any suggestions?'

Sophia and Mary looked straight at him. With a deadpan mood, Sophia retorted, 'Stick him in a cannon and fire the shot back to France?'

The King smiled, 'Aye, that's a good girl. We'll show him!' He dawdled in his thoughts when suddenly an odd Idea popped into His head. 'I know, we'll set the Rose on him. That should teach him not to mess about in Europe. She can strangle him with her thorny disposition.'

The sisters stared at one another, then at His Majesty. 'I did not think Miss Rose has a thorny disposition,' Sophia stated.

'She doesn't, unless cross... or if you discuss anything to do with That Place her mother used to live in.'

'Oh yes,' Mary recalled, 'That would surely piss her off. Napoleon would be toasted!'

'And with plenty of butter too, no doubt,' The King suggested, laughing.

'That is the soundest Idea you have had in years, Papa,' Mary declared.

His Majesty got up. 'Right, that is settled. Fetch my secretary. There is going to be a Wrestling Match.'

The Princesses left The King to the harpsichord, where He continued playing the endless Handel pieces recalled from memory. He had a sly grin on His face... *this will be a Mad Gamble, but if we win, it can put an end to the War and bring Peace to Europe.*

* * * * * *

I, meanwhile, was in the Company of the Prince, who had heard about the news regarding Waterloo. The word had spread and the Prince, with a copy sent to The King, had received a desperate correspondence from Napoleon himself, who wrote:

To Your Most Merciful British Majesty and Highness:
Please Please PLEASE have mercy on me. I am so sorry for wanting to invade your wonderful country of shopkeepers and for raiding the various lands of Europe in order to spread my Crazy New-Order Notions. I beseech you not to do me nor my family any harm. I know I had been your Most Greatest Enemy, but let Bygones be Bygones. Most of all, PLEASE DO NOT HUMILIATE ME FURTHER BY IMPOSING A WRESTLING MATCH AGAINST A MERE GIRL! I will be the Laughing Stock of the World.
Yours Faithfully,
NB

The Prince put the letter in his coat pocket. 'The man's a laughing stock anyway, and *that* is the point. Besides, I have his favourite desk, ha-ha,' he said, looking at me, 'You know Boney's scared of you.'

'Why should he be scared of me?'

'Because Papa and I gave a description of you to Wellington who passed it on to his Generals who passed it onto Boney and now the poor man's shitting himself.'

'The old Chinese whisper trick?'

'You got it; the more exotic, the better, I always say.'

'You do know Napoleon is committing Treason, sir,' I stated.

'My dear, that is why they call it a Revolution and it must End. Now. With You at the Helm.'

I blushed volumes at Prinny's remark and confidence in me. Usually, worldly affairs of state were not solved via a wrestling match, but since The King ordered it and, as everyone was in concordance with the idea, it will take place. As there was no real 'battle' as such, this business with Europe had to be decided in a better way. The Prince saw himself as a figurehead, and not an interference... let these affairs be left to the Government, with the exception of the Matter regarding Napoleon. In reality, His Highness was having too much fun teasing me regarding the Dishy Servant, Mr Elderfynne.

Chapter XVIII

Elderfynne had received a letter for the Prince. It was from The King and, even though everyone thought Him Mad, He was still capable of writing correspondence... with a little help from a servant or a stay-at-home Daughter.

As he gave it to the Prince, the Royal burst out, 'Blast it, what does Papa want now? God, He can be such a nuisance. Can't He just let me get on with it??'

'I would not know, sir, I do not serve Him,' Elderfynne replied in a dour tone.

'Yes, yes, I know,' the Prince dismissed the comment, opening and reading the message, 'It confirms there is to be a wrestling match between Cynthia Rose Woodes-Hastings and Napoleon Bonaparte... I know about this, but,' the Prince's eyes bulged out, similar to The King's, 'Wickett, what is my Mad Father thinking?? Is He totally ungovernable???'

'Your Highness, it seems that Your Father has high esteem for Miss Rose to pit her against the Formidable Enemy of Europe.'

'She could be Humiliated and have More to Worry About than the history of her mother! I mean, Napoleon??!!!' The Prince was flabbergasted and most perturbed.

'That would only be if she loses. If she wins, well, well, then Our Rose would bring an end to the War and possibly have the French Royals restored.'

'If... they had not been killed off first.'

'I heard they fled to Austria, sir.'

'Austria?' The Prince was puzzled.

'Yes. They wore disguises... they made themselves look and smell like peasants. The problem was, the whiff was so bad, it gagged out the whole party, as well as anyone who *could* recognise them, never mind a portrait on a coin. It took awhile to sort out. Anyway, Antoinette's brother rules there as Joseph II. He'd given them sanctuary,' Elderfynne recollected.

There was a pause and Elderfynne continued, 'Do you think Miss Rose would do it?'

'I believe she will,' the Prince grinned, 'She'd better, she knows she Serves Us; 'tis no different than a soldier going off to War.'

'Or a Young Lady of Good Standing participating in a Wrestling Match with the most Dangerous Entity on the Planet.'

'Nah, it's not that bad, Wickett.'

'Hmm... maybe it should be You, Your Highness, who fights the Napoleon. I mean, you can invite him over here to Brighton, bedazzle him with Your Exotic Tastes in Decor, showing him the dizzying patterns of the wallpaper. Then, have him stay for dinner, where you feed him one of your Most Lavish Banquets you could create, with plenty of Wine, of course. When the poor man is drunk with sleep and filled in the belly, you then imprison him. Once in the prison, your Father treat him to His Daily Concerts in the cell. If that does not get Napoleon to capitulate to Our Terms, well, then I cannot fathom what will.'

'John Pickwick Elderfynne?' The Prince used his valet's full name.

'Yes, sir?'

'That is the most cruellest notion I had ever heard. No one should be subject to Papa's private renditions of Handel or any other composer, not even Napoleon! No. You, Wickett, will inform Miss Rose of her Duty and bring her to me. I must have her trained for the event. She must not fail or we *ALL* fail.'

'As you command, Your Highness,' Elderfynne answered.

'Actually, perhaps we can use some of your idea. Let us win the match first.'

Elderfynne grinned as he exited the room.

* * * * * *

It was thus set that I was to enter into a Wrestling Match with Napoleon. The Prince hired a sportsman who had experience in the genre and I was to perform gruelling exercises in the meantime to allow my body to become Fitter toward its Endurance. Much of my plans to help the Prince had been put on hold as this was Our Priority. I spent many hours in the day in a separate room with the trainer working very hard on the goal.

Soon enough, we went London, where Napoleon was being held prisoner. The Tower of London was the place the Government kept the fellow before my upcoming Confrontation with him. Once a Royal Residence, the Tower still had usable apartments which our party took advantage of. There were plenty of dungeons for criminals and Traitors of State to be detained. In the apartment once used by an ancient King, the Prince bunked myself with Elderfynne, and he took the room next door.

I noticed a small privy besides the main bedroom I was to sleep in. There was an impression of a cross in the wall, and I wondered about it... I reckoned it was a chapel during a more religious period of English history. However, as it represented the Old Faith, modern-day guests felt the space would be better used for Convenience's Sake.

It was a long trip (it seemed) from Brighton and I flopped on the bed besides Elderfynne, who was sitting on the bed, removing his boots.

'Agh, that's better,' he exhaled, 'God, it is so hot in here. My dear, could you please open the window?'

'Sure thing,' I said, getting up to open that 'chapel' privy window. A fresh breeze blew in and it was most relieving.

'Do pardon me,' Elderfynne joined me in the privy, reaching for the Pot. I excused myself and went to unpack my clothes.

Not wanting to seem un-gentlemanly, he asked, 'Miss Rose, are you in Need of the Pot?'

Christ, I was so busy about myself, I forgot about that. I figured to give it a go.

'Sorry about the odour, but one must do...,' he said.

'... what one must do, I know,' I finished the sentence for him. I tried it out and it felt good. I returned the pot to its place once it had been emptied.

'One would think there would be a washbasin somewhere,' I whinged, 'After all, a King once lived here!'

'I will see if I can sort that out for you, Miss Rose.' *Elderfynne was so accommodating.*

We spent the evening with the Royals as Guests, not servants, at St. James' Palace. The Prince's daughter, Charlotte was present. I got an opportunity to quickly meet with her among other notables who dined with us. There was a ball planned as well where I was able to dance with many people, including Elderfynne. I really enjoyed the Company and thought it gave a good shot of morale for me on the Morrow of Execution. Well, it would be if I lose against the French Leader. Many wished me luck. Some doubted my ability. The King Himself voiced His Opinion quite Assertively, for someone who everybody thought was *mad*.

He announced to all, 'I have a Great Confidence in Cynthia Rose. If she is anything like her mother, Bonaparte will be finished for good! The War will be Over and Our Shores will remain Silent with Contentment, whilst we enjoy Our Imperial Spoils.'

There was a murmuring which hushed when the music played again. It was Handel, The King's favourite composer. *At least this time, it was not The King playing!*

We spent our time into the evening and then we rode back to the Tower. The Prince wished me luck and bade me a good night... winking at me in the process because I was in the same room as *the Dishy Servant.*

'He's a good Lad, Miss Rose; he'll do you no harm,' the Prince assured.

'Gee, thanks,' I rolled my eyes.

Elderfynne was getting out of his suit when I walked in. He hurried to a screen panel and carried on changing behind it.

'And I thought only women were bashful,' I sighed.

'It's not you, my dear, it's just...,' he came out, wearing only his shift, holding the rest of his apparel.

'Don't worry, I won't look if you don't. Did you ask the Prince about the water?'

'I had time tonight and the Guards of the Tower had provided us with the basin and a huge jug of water which can be refilled at any time. So, we must take care in using it.'

'Thanks,' I looked in the privy to see the basin, which I confess not noticing before. 'I must ask you, if you do not mind... what would you like to be called?'

'The Prince calls me Wickett, as you know; but you may call me... hmmm,' he thought a moment, 'How about Fynn? Just between us, of course, so as to delay confusion.'

'I think that would be fine with me... Fynn,' I giggled, changing out of the tarty dress I wore to the dinner/dance.

I did not bother with the screen panel and just undressed. I did not care who was looking. I did cover the Modesty, but I had no squeamishness for the Other Regions.

'You are a beautiful girl, Miss Rose,' Fynn declared.

'I think you're quite the dish, too. In fact His Majesty and His Highness were trying to put us together, for some odd reason or t'other.'

'I am aware of Their Majesties doings. I was told about you too and was most eager to meet your Acquaintance.'

So, it fell on both sides. 'I think Miss Rose is too formal, don't you think?'

'How about CynRose?'

'Weird!'

'Got any other solutions?'

'Nah, I was just kidding.'

'Come, we'll to bed, and then, you have an appointment with Destiny.'

I looked at Fynn. *Cheeky so and so, but lovable.*

'So it's good night, then.'

'You've a Big Day Ahead of you. Come, dear.' He patted the bed.

I hesitated, as I never slept with a Man before, let alone sleeping with someone who resembled... *Father. Eugh!* Yet, I did secretly find him Most Attractive, and Father was quite a Looker himself. *No wonder Mother packed up and fled into his Arms and Country!*

I got into the bed with Fynn. Wow, this was a soft bed... fit for a King... *wait, but we're Servants... I guess I must have been the Person of the Moment to get such a place to sleep as this.* I gave Fynn a kiss which he returned. I held him in my arms and lightly fondled him. He did so with me, but we wanted to save the Important Part of Ourselves for *another time.*

As I was nodding, a poetic thought crept upon me:

Lo, I bed ye for the Night,
And you are holding me so tight.
When the Fire's Fossils seek their Light,
I shall not be Afraid.

After a good cuddling, I passed the night in well-earned sleep.

The next morning brought birds singing near the chapel-privy window, which we left open during the night. It made it cooler and as we were high up, we were unbothered by any Undesirable Wanderers who would be lurking in the night.

After a hearty breakfast with the Prince, who had our meals brought to us in our Chambers, I began to get ready. We went outside into another area of the Tower, where a place was prepared specifically for the Event. I wore something that resembled undergarments, without a stay and very lightweight. My golden blonde hair was pulled back pretty tightly into a bun with the loose ends tucked away. I think I was ready, but felt insecure about this situation. I accepted it, prayed silently for Deliverance and Victory and kissed Fynn for luck.

'I wish you all the best CynRose,' he said, 'My prayers and thoughts are with you.'

'It is much appreciated. Thank you,' I gave him another kiss.

The Prince watched us, 'Oooh, is he Striking your Fancy, now? Don't forget, you're to Win for Us!'

'I know.' *God, I did not need continual reminding.*

I entered the arena and Napoleon was in his Corner, sneering at me.

'So, I am to fight against this slip of a girl? C'est Mademoiselle?' He gave a laugh I could not forget. I had to think and concentrated on how to bring him down. *Was all the training worth it?*

We soon faced one another... it was hot in the room, with all the people and the windows were high up where were fought. I nearly choked with a stifling feeling, but instead, I experienced something else... *sweat dripping from my head, down past my neck, along my back and into the rear. The front piece of my outfit was imprisoned with wetness. The whole of my body had anticipated the full weight of a man not much taller than myself.*

'You're sweating,' Napoleon taunted me.

I did not answer. The crowd was bloodthirsty for my Opponent's Defeat and I had to deliver. They wanted his head, if not a banquet made up solely of *him*. There were many a high personage present at the fight, such as the Royals, members of Parliament, some military figures such as Nelson and Wellington. Wellington was the one who led the Capture of Napoleon, near the small area of Waterloo in the Netherlands. Nelson took a break from the Canal Waterworks with Emma to witness the potential defeat of the one whose Navy had a go at his at Trafalgar. He wanted Napoleon out of the picture entirely... *he vehemently hated him and his Republican ideas and, as one could guess, he was not the only one.* All present had High Stakes in the Matter and the Matter was to End the Menagerie of Chaos.

I grabbed Napoleon by the throat and desperately tried to lower him into submission. All the weeks of training had helped me, but *what was it*, I'd wondered, *that gave me such a strength to make a man like him kneel?*

I had no chance to think, when suddenly, he grabbed me, pulling me upwards and upside down. Luckily, my Modesty was surely intact, but then he unceremoniously threw me onto the floor of the arena. He strode around me like a strutting cock in a hen house.

A few in the crowd shouted and cheered me on, though I had heard some others cheer for Napoleon, who waved to the crowd. I got up and bounced on him, as he fell to the floor. I clapped and mocked him, as he got up, looking like a raging fire inside a bull's body. He rushed toward me and I got out of the way, so he collided with the ropes surrounding our domain. Momentum took over as Napoleon was pushed backward into the centre. He came to, after the initial light-headedness and saw me waiting for another go. He hollered, running toward me and I got out of the way so he can collide with the ropes, again.

Now, Napoleon was fuming mad. A short break was called and he went into his corner to get refreshment and I went into mine for the same.

The Prince came up to me, 'You're doing fine, Cynthia. You will trounce Bonaparte and bring an End to this.'

The King, waiting behind him, drooling on a front cloth, had gained some clarity. 'Do us proud, Cynthia Rose. I believe in you and, like your mother, you will Defeat the Enemy, what what!' He carried on drooling as an attendant returned Him to His seat. His Brain may be fading, yet the Kind Sentiment remained present.

Fynn, too, wished me well. I looked at him fondly and realised I had to Win. It was not just Europe that was at Stake. I really wanted him and if I lost, I feared I would lose him... *after all, who wants to date or marry a Loser?*

'Go get him, Cynthia,' the Prince called out to me as I regained my place in the forum.

Elderfynne whispered to the Prince, 'This is it.'

'You're right, Wickett. If we screw this up, it will be the end of Civilisation as We Know It.'

'Yea, perhaps it will not be Civilised at all.'

'That is why it is called 'The End', *duh!*'

Elderfynne knew his Place from there. He silently rooted for me to win, though not as obviously and boorishly as his counterparts did.

I heard all the chants, shouts and cheers from all sides. It all went to my head, but I refrained from being too cocky about it, for I was told in the training about being too overconfident. I took my time, examining the beast within me, and staring at the beast everyone present wanted to see dead. Napoleon and I were at a stand still, just eyeing one another to see who would make the first move.

I did not have to wait long as Napoleon rushed at me, boasting, 'You are toast, and so is your little country, too.'

'We will see about that, Monsieur Blownaparte.'

'You've no gun fire in your arsenal to defeat me, Mademoiselle.'

'You have not seen me angry,' I retorted.

He lunged and toppled me over, grabbing my arm and pulling it backward. *God, that hurt!*

I was nearly paralysed and could not get up. The bastard nearly got me, when I looked up to see the Prince and his Entourage smiling and waving at me. It gave me the Confidence I needed at the time.

I then moved my torso up and down to unbalance Napoleon off me. (not that it took much to unbalance *this* French Leader). Soon, I freed myself from him and we faced each other, again. The crowd roared around us and the atmosphere intensified.

Napoleon began to speak to me, 'I bet your mother did not tell you everything about herself.'

'I was told enough. She was a Colonist who served The King and defeated the American Colonial Rebellion.' I grabbed his arm and twisted it behind his back.

'I heard she was ill-raised.'

The words came into my mind like a steam iron to fabric. I was not amused and I prayed the dumbfuck would not continue this line of conversation. I remembered what Father had told me before he died. I also thought about Father himself and what a Good Man he was. *The Soldier, who rescued my mother; my mother, who rescued the Colonies from themselves to regain their Royal senses.* I could not take it any longer and I put more pressure upon his arm, hopeful I can get it to the point of breaking.

Napoleon cracked on, even more cruelly than ever, 'I also heard she was a J-.'

'NO!' I screamed outward, slamming his face to the floor. I got on his back and bounced on his spine 'til he was forcibly pinned down. He was unable to utter or taunt me any further.

I took the opportunity to put this right and yelled, 'She had no choice. She made the decision to leave that family and is no longer associated with them. She was not one of them, nor am I one of them. We got the tie legally unbound, and *YOU ARE DEAD WRONG!*'

And with that, I slammed his face to the ground once more. I saw blood coming out and a countdown had commenced. Napoleon was shattered by this time, but recklessly tried to topple me off him. He failed, but not without turning toward me to peer at me viciously with evil eyes, hissing and baying for my blood. His nose looked a right mess but at least *his* blood had congealed. I blithely spat at the fellow, saliva caked all over his Corsican mush.

'Arugh!' He cried out in anguish.

The referee concluded, '3-2-1. We have a winner... Cynthia Rose Woodes-Hastings.'

The crowded went wild and cheered relentlessly. The referee had held my arm up in Victory.

Napoleon regained himself, wiped off my handiwork and bellowed, 'Ah, phooey on you and your stupid country of booksellers.' He walked off to his corner, sulking. After this event, I never saw the fellow again.

The Prince ran to give me a hug. 'How do you feel?'

I looked at him point blank, 'Carême-cracker'd!'

He laughed so hard, he hardly could contain his joy toward my joke, 'Do you know what this means?!'

'I think I have a pretty good idea, Prinny,' I exhaled after being released from his embrace.

The King came along and joined in, 'I think I have a good idea, too, what what!' However, His lucidness was more than one could bear. 'You spat at him, didn't you? One couldn't help but notice.'

I had not realised anyone had seen The Handiwork.

'I beg Forgiveness, Your Majesty, but the damn sod brought up my mother and her time in the Colonies... even recalling her previous affiliation to which she had violently objected and rejected in the end. I had to Defend her and shut him up!'

'You are quite right in your Doing,' the Prince comforted, 'Remember, Bonaparte's tactics were not at all agreeable, either, so you are in Good Company. You did what you had to do, like a true combatant.'

'Amen. Cynthia, you are very courageous, just like your mother. She would have been proud of you,' The King said, then He turned to His attendant, 'Help me to the carriage,' and they walked off.

Fynn came up to me, 'You did well, my dear. You stopped a terrible regime from continuing.'

'You would not want to be under his yoke, believe me,' I answered.

'I do not think one would.'

The Duke of Wellington came up to congratulate me, sticking his hand out. I shook his hand and looked at him. He was far nobler than his portraits revealed and his nose stood out, larger than life.

I found it so difficult to believe *he* was not chosen to wrestle with Napoleon. *It would have been a better match... I'd also heard wresting was one of King Louis XVI's hobbies!* Between these illustrious fellows, I still could not understand why *I* was chosen to fight Bonaparte.

Wellington looked around, feeling a redundancy he's never felt before. Then he said aloud, not to anyone in particular, 'Well, that's that. I'm off to Parliament now. I am going into Politics.' He hastily retreated toward his New Calling.

Chapter XIX

After the Match, I returned to Brighton with Prinny's entourage. An idea was hatched in the carriage to plan for a Banquet to honour my Victory over Napoleon.

'Why don't we invite all of Brighton to it? It would outwardly show your Kind Intention to the Great Populace,' I suggested.

Prinny snuffled into his tin, a Habit, I am hoping to Remove from his Routines. 'So you are willing to allow riff-raff invade my Beautiful Pavilion?'

I had to think fast, 'They could remain outside where they can be allowed refreshments from the Banquet. The excessive amounts of Your Party Foods are worth parting from and be divided amongst the Starving Masses. You would be looked upon fondly as someone who looks after all, just as a King would, I might well add! Those people probably had not eaten for weeks.'

The Prince scoffed, ''Tis a wonder they remain Alive, then.' He turned Thoughtful (*a miracle indeed!*), but retained his Prejudice. 'We will keep them at a distance. Our grounds have plenty of space and the Rear Gardens may be an ideal for their Moment in the Sun. Of course, it shall be heavily guarded.'

'Discreetly, though. One mustn't threaten them... especially in a uniform to which they may find disgust,' I further added.

He agreed with me, 'Quite right, lass. We shall dress our Guards undercover, the way the French Royals escaped into Austria.'

'Sir, do recall, they had to duplicate not just the look, but the odour of such.'

He pondered, 'Can't be helped, can't be helped. Anyway, they'll all be outside. Plenty of space to whiff about in, eh eh?'

I suspected Prinny was beginning to continue the Mannerisms of The King, despite his Earlier Denouncements of the Same. I was unsure if it was due to Genuine Affection, or just a Colourful Jest. At this point, we reached the Pavilion and everybody took leave of the carriage.

Elderfynne was walking behind us and cautiously snuck up behind me. 'CynRose?'

I turned around and responded, 'Fynn?'

'Forgive me, but I hadn't sufficient time to congratulate you personally on your Napoleonic success.'

I giggled, and felt proud someone took time to notice me and my Efforts for the State. The Prince grinned wildly and put his arm around me.

Fynn continued, 'I am hoping, after that first night betwixt us, that we shall have many more. I trust you enjoyed yourself?'

'You nay harmed me, Fynn,' I assured him. The Prince let go of me, gloating that his and his Family's handiwork had paid off. I gave Fynn a hug, 'I confess a slight, as it was not enough.'

'Not enough for what?'

I gave Fynn a deep kiss and walked toward my suites.

'Well, well, well,' Prinny cooed, 'So are you in love, Wickett?'

He gave the Prince a doe-eyed look and bowed. He went into the Pavilion to refresh himself and attend to his duties.

I guess Papa's oddities worked in our favour, the Prince reflected, as he followed the lovers to prepare for the upcoming Event.

* * * * * *

We spent the next several days making plans for that Banquet. Many other ones were held around the country to celebrate Napoleon's Defeat. However, for Napoleon, there was nothing to celebrate. He was removed from the Tower and under Heavy Guard, was sent abroad to the lonely fortress at Sur-Le-Merde, on the coast of France. A neighbouring pig farm had kept the prisoners busy over the centuries, and luckily for Napoleon, the farm was still in use.

The officers and common soldier guards who brought over the Defeated decided to rename the surrounding district after the place Wellington had him captured, Waterloo. As this was France, it was jokingly translated into Loo de L'Eau and the name stuck indefinitely.

Once there, Napoleon was not given any comforts. He wore plain, boring, monochrome white linen with accompanying trousers and boots, the latter sorely needed for his New Occupation. At least, the clothes were cleaned and changed on a daily basis. There is Imprisonment, of course, and then there is Cruelty. One can only go so far. However, Fynn's earlier plan, regarding putting an amateur musician in the cell to mimic George III's renditions of Handel, proved to be far worse than a dirty shift could offer... *especially when the musician could not sing, either.*

He spent the rest of his natural life working on the pig farm, getting up close and personal with his Charges. Napoleon fell over one time and, during the process of getting up, he was face to face with one of the many pigs. It grunted in his face and another pig came up from behind and Let Go. The results had put the poor man in a true *L'Etat de Merde* and this proved he was no better than anyone else anymore. Passers by were fascinated how such a Lofty Fellow had gotten so Far Down in Society... *and by an English noblewoman, too!* The town was alit with the news and one could not help but laugh.

* * * * * *

Meanwhile, the chefs were busy in the kitchen with all the foodstuffs to be ordered and served. Fynn was checking the cutlery, crockery and glassware, with a crew beneath him polishing the lot to keep them looking their best.

I kept my place with the Prince, who needed emotional comfort and would have leaned toward something unruly. He had done large Parties similar, but nothing like this. It made him a bit unnerved and he ran to his snuffbox. I took it from him and scolded him strongly.

'You're right,' he surrendered and pouted.

'You are giving a Big Show and this could Make or Break you in Brighton. You need to be a Sport of it and show you can be just a good as a King as your Father.'

'But I am not like him.'

I wanted to rap him 'cross the face for that repetitious comment.

'That is what you need to rise above. You are the Prince; the next step for you is King. You might well get ready for it. You are just as good as He was, maybe better cos you are younger and people would look up to you more so,' I added.

'Pressure's on, then.'

'It might not be as bad as you think, Your Highness.'

The Prince glared at me for using his Title when we've become more informal. I gave him a supportive hug.

'I guess this would do, instead of snuff, Miss Rose,' he said, mockingly reverting to formality as I had. 'I am sorry.'

'Forget about it.'

* * * * * *

When the day finally arrived, there were people queuing outside. The 'Guards', as we referred to them, had seen which ones remained for the outdoor party and those allowed inside. The difference was noticeable and the Great Masses were shown through the beautiful Rear Gardens, where the food was waiting for them.

Those who were Privileged to go inside were greeted with the Prince looking and acting his Best... just as a King would. As I told him before, this would be good practise. His welcome and warmth about him impressed many. It surprised everyone as they admired the Eastern-styled Decor throughout the ground floor.

An anonymous participant queried, 'Is that the wanton Prince everyone accuses of spending thousands of public monies to suit his Own Purposes?'

Another answered him, 'Apparently so... there is that Woodes-Hastings girl who'd been helping His Highness come to his senses. This banquet is for her, I believe and all of Brighton is here for this.'

'Wow, but not only that, she'd even beaten Bonaparte in that wrestling match,' said the first fellow, as he commenced eating.

The other person smiled and ate, thinking about the Current Circumstances of the Former Dictator.

The Prince's daughter, Charlotte and her suitor, Leopold of Coburg had come too. They were keen to meet up with His Highness. The Prince's wife, Caroline, had long been separated from him and led a completely different life on her own; thus, she was not present. The rest of the Royal family were either serving abroad, getting married and/or moving abroad, and in The King and Queen's case, ailing.

The people inside were brought into one of the vast Public Rooms in the Pavilion. They marvelled at the Chinese dragon imagery on the walls and ceiling, most thinking that it could pop out and fly out at them at any second, breathing heavy fire.

The Prince took me over to his daughter and the suitor. We shook hands, happy to rekindle the acquaintance... though I never met Leopold.

'Ah, we meet again. We've heard about that match you were in. It was so-much-talked about. The news ran faster than a horse,' Princess Charlotte said.

'Maybe they will invent something that will be faster,' I quipped.

'Perhaps the recently attempted steam-oriented technology could show us the way,' Leopold observed.

'So, how do you like working for Papa?' Charlotte wondered.

'It is like working with The King, only more fun. He's like a boy, you know, but shows his full maturity when needed,' I replied.

'Papa has a Reputation, you know,' she smiled at me.

'I know, that is why The King sent me here.'

Leopold interjected, 'I noticed there are marquees outside. Is there something we are missing out on?'

'Oh, they're for the commoners, the starving, the homeless and the hopeless. It is a gesture toward them the Prince is not the Knock-Around Layabout everybody thinks he is.'

'A marketing ploy! Good Good,' Leopold commented.

I never thought of it that way, but if this shows the Prince in the Best Light, then, let it.

'Do you know there is a Ball later on,' Charlotte reminded me.

My eyes widened and I stared at the Prince... *I had not known.*

'Surprise,' His Highness said, taking out his monocle and regarding the clock beside him.

'I must change, umm... where's Fynn?'

'Who?' Charlotte asked.

'Elderfynne, that Dishy Servant you Lot placed before me for Romantic Purposes.'

'Ah, him,' she grinned.

'What?' Leopold looked confused. Charlotte told him about how The King was trying to match me with Elderfynne and that there was a bit of Love between us. Leopold nodded in acknowledgement.

'Why don't you get changed, Miss Rose. I'll have your Fynn beside you in no time,' the Prince spoke formally at me, keeping the Appearance, due to the Event.

'Alright,' I claimed departure and went to my suite to change.

The Prince, Charlotte and Leopold stayed together as people were walking up to them and giving them usual Royally accepted gestures of curtsies and bows.

'This is some Party,' Leopold said to the Prince.

'It was Our Idea. We were coming home from London and thought of it in the carriage.'

Charlotte asked, 'Was it your idea to invite the Populace?'

'Look at me, daughter! What do you think?'

She was taken aback and realised his Reputation would not allow him to do anything this Christian.

'So, whose was it then?' Her interrogation went on.

'Miss Rose's of course.'

Everyone filed into the adjacent ballroom and musicians were setting up on a higher level, ready to play their assigned pieces.

I returned to the Party, looking very rich in a pink satin gown I brought with me for such a purpose. My hair was set up in the back with queued curls at the sides. I hoped I would get a chance with Fynn, as I could now see him for genuine.

The Prince came up to me. 'I've given Wickett the night off. You can have your wicked way with him, and have the time to get to know one another.'

'Thank you,' I kissed him on the cheek. *I thought that would be enough.* 'Where is he, if I may ask?'

'Clearing up tables at the moment. His off-time had not begun because I still need every Servant for the moment. Go up and dance with someone. Don't worry, he'll be along.'

I stood alone as I watched the others dance. I reflected on all that happened to me of late and felt good about it. *I was proud to live up to the name, Woodes-Hastings.*

Suddenly an aging uniformed chap came up to me, 'May I have this dance, miss?'

'Certainly, sir.' I extended my arm for him to hold and we joined in with the rest.

'So you are The Rose Who Beat Napoleon?'

Blushing, I remarked, 'Yes, yes, I am.' *I felt so bashful.*

'I bet it did you good with all the moves you made upon him.'

'It did not do me good, per se, but it was welcoming once I pinned him down for good.'

'Was it more than just a trouncing... did he turn you on?'

'Umm...,' I paused, 'No, he did not 'turn me on' as you put it.'

'So you did not fancy him, then... being so close and very personal.'

'Look, I was there to beat him and to end the War. I wasn't trying to get social with the fellow,' I snapped.

'I must apologise, miss, you know how soldiers talk. I meant no offence.'

'My loyalty is to His Majesty. He is who I serve.'

'And rightly so; as do I, and as did your father, if I am correct in your identity,' the gentlemen concurred.

'You knew my father?'

'You're Cynthia Rose Woodes-Hastings, right?'

'Aye, that I am.'

'I served with your father. I am Captain Cateliffe. He was one of my dearest friends. We served in the Colonies together. I was part of the rescue mission to remove your mother from the family who abused her and who were suspected of Sedition against His Majesty. I am sure you are aware of what happened.'

'Father had a heart to heart with me before he died.'

'In setting her free, we had to kill a lot of people that night. There was a local Indian tribe who assisted us.'

'Wow,' I was gob struck. I asked the Captain if we could sit down for awhile and talk. He was happy to oblige.

We sat in the back on one of the benches. Swirling gowns and coattails flew 'round like birds.

'I trust you have many questions,' Cateliffe said.

'Well, I was told much, but not in detail, as I do not feel it befitting to me. My life is very different from hers and I would like to keep it that way. I understood she held the Colonies with Contempt.'

'Aye, that she did. However, the colonists had kicked off again. In 1812, they disregarded and disrespected our rule by invading Canada. We had to go in as reinforcements and many of us had perished in the assault. Most of them friends of mine and your father's. Buckingham and Nay-Smith, my best mates, were among the casualties. I am the last of your father's group, as it were.'

'My, my,' I was astounded. It was fascinating to see someone who survived... *there was always one, or a few survivors. I never thought I would get to meet one.*

'Negotiations began to give Independence to the colonies. I think the forty years or so since their last attempt had cooled them slightly, so we parted more amicably. They can still trade with us, but are no longer part of Our Empire and have no wish to be.'

'Bastards don't know what they're missing,' I snorted.

'Their tough luck... anyway, your mother knew better and that is why you are here,' Cateliffe reassured.

'Mothers always know better anyway cos they've got experience.'

'Apparently, not all mothers have it, though. Look at your mother's family.'

'I would rather not, thank you. They were an exception... *to everything.*'

I sighed and further reflected. The headiness of the party was getting to me. Cateliffe offered me a drink, which I accepted. He left me for a few moments when Fynn finally arrived.

'My dear CynRose,' he greeted.

'Fynn,' I stood up to kiss him. *That felt good.*

Cateliffe returned from the bar with my drink and he saw Elderfynne.

It was obvious there was a relapse in memory... *I guessed all soldiers had it.* 'Willec?'

'Who?' Fynn turned to face the old soldier, looking perplexed.

I rushed in to assist, 'Mr Elderfynne, this is Captain Cateliffe of His Majesty's Forces, Totteringstate Regiment. The only survivor of Father's best friends.' I was crestfallen when saying the last bit.

'How do you do, sir,' Fynn extended his hand.

Cateliffe put his drink down on a table, 'Hello, nice to meet you. You look ever-so-much-like him.'

'Well, I confess I am a relation, a very distant, far off and away relation. We shared the same ancestor.'

'You don't say? Who, may I presume was the fellow?'

It was not Fynn's way to share this matter with others, especially with strangers. Luckily, the Prince turned up and the topic was shelved for the moment. There was a quick buzz of introduction and Fynn and I excused ourselves for the next dance.

The Prince watched on, reflecting his thoughts to Cateliffe, 'Father was right. Those two make a sprightly couple.'

'This was your Father's doing? The King?'

'Yes.'

'They remind me of when Willec and Cynthia the Elder got together way back in the Colonies. I am so glad we let the Colonies go.'

'Eventually, my dear Cateliffe, we all must think for ourselves. It is whether or not other people wish to hear our thoughts, which is the rub.'

'It was so long ago,' he carried on reminiscing.

The Prince concurred and left the Old Soldier to his Reveries.

I remained with Fynn for the remainder of the evening and long into the night. Together, we did our Forever Dance.